Fatal Facts

Other Avalon Books by Jill Giencke

STILL WATERS
SECRETS OF ECHO MOON

FATAL ◊ FACTS

JILL GIENCKE

AVALON BOOKS

THOMAS BOUREGY AND COMPANY, INC.
401 LAFAYETTE STREET
NEW YORK, NEW YORK 10003

© Copyright 1993 by Jill Giencke
Library of Congress Catalog Card Number: 92-97354
ISBN 0-8034-8976-5

PRINTED IN THE UNITED STATES OF AMERICA
ON ACID-FREE PAPER
BY HADDON CRAFTSMEN, SCRANTON, PENNSYLVANIA

To Grandma Marcella with every affection

Chapter One

I snapped on my turn signal, checked the rearview mirror, and moved into the right lane. Up ahead, visible between each swish of the wiper blades, a faded wooden sign indicated the entrance to Lunham College. A long, tree-lined avenue led to the main building, and I drove down it slowly, my head swiveling to take in my new surroundings.

All the rain certainly made things appear gloomy. The dark trees standing sentinel beside the road waved branches filled with leaves already turning although it was only the middle of September. A deep-gray sky hung over the scene and, as the college came into view, a brief flash of lightning illuminated the cluster of cream brick buildings.

Nothing was going to dampen my enthusiasm, though. I was looking forward to today, to my new job. I was determined to be the best archivist Lunham had ever seen. "Or die trying," I joked aloud, little realizing how true those words would be.

1

Swinging my car into one of the many vacant spots in the lot, I switched off the engine and glanced at my watch. Nine-fourteen. I was early for my nine-thirty appointment. Well, that was good. All those résumé books said being early made a good impression with the boss, and that couldn't hurt.

I flipped down the visor, taking one last look in the mirror there. My lipstick, a lovely shade of dark pink, had miraculously stayed on for the half-mile journey from my flat to the college. The freckles on my cheeks, which blossom into full view each summer, were barely visible, a fact I noted with pleasure. There are some folks who think freckles are darling, and they are— on eight-year-olds. On twenty-eight-year-olds like me, however, the effect is a bit less endearing. Still, with fair skin and a reddish tint in my hair, I always knew they were inevitable. I smiled at my reflection, trying to look both friendly and professional.

"Hello. I'm Rose Claypool," I rehearsed. "It's so good to be here." Ugh! Who would ever believe such a sappy line, even if it was the truth?

"Hi! I'm Rose!" Nope, too casual.

"Thanks so much for giving me a job and getting me out of a bad situation." That would never do. Too honest.

In the end, I gathered up my nearly empty briefcase and my blue-plaid umbrella, slammed the car door on the hem of my trench coat, groaned, wrenched the coat free, hoisted the umbrella, and walked rapidly in the direction of the main entrance.

The building was a sprawling one, three stories high, extending about one hundred feet in either direction from the big front doors. It was set in a huge, grassy clearing, like some cathedral in rural England. Any other time it would have struck me as picturesque. Now, with my unaccustomed high heels pinching my toes and the rain coming down in ever heavier sheets, all I could think of was how much more sidewalk I had to cover before getting indoors.

Hastening up the ten steps to the big double doors, I felt one heel slip on the slick pavement, teetered a bit, and swung my umbrella out as I regained my balance. The feel of the heavy metal door handle beneath my hand was welcome. I hurried inside.

The umbrella collapsed easily enough, and I gave it a brisk shake, scattering raindrops over the black rubber mat on the lobby floor.

Looking around me, I realized this main entryway acted as a huge landing on a flight of wide steps. Above me, on what must be the first floor, I could see an open reception area with heavy, decorative pillars supporting a ceiling of detailed wooden panels. Inlaid tiles on the floor depicted the college emblem—a glowing candlestick—and the school motto. I knew from the most recent class bulletin what the letters circling the candle would spell. "Truth conquers." An inspiring sentiment.

From below, I could hear the echo of many conversations and the high pitch of female laughter. *The student body seems cheery enough,* I thought, and, although I'd always rather be around laughing, happy people than brooding intellectuals, I turned my back on the lively sounds and mounted the steps to the first floor.

A heavy sense of quiet surrounded me as I paused at the top of the staircase, and I fought the urge to tiptoe across the floor. The air was thick and dull here, ample evidence that the new semester had just begun. Three months of stale, uncirculated air lingered, not yet dispelled by air-conditioning or heating systems. The fresh smell of the rain still clung to me, however, and I welcomed the contrast.

Long hallways stretched in either direction of the open space. I knew I'd have to go searching for the administrative offices soon, but first I took a moment to admire that lovely ceiling overhead and trailed my hand across one of the cool, ivory pillars. If I stretched, both arms might have circled it, I think, but I've never put that hypothesis to the test.

A set of three matching doors to my right were headed with a sign labeled *Auditorium*, and a series of glass-fronted display cases rimmed the area. Lighted from within, the cases were filled with little treasures. At a glance, I spotted vases, statues, and other sculpture, and I made a mental note to take a closer look in the near future.

The sharp, shrill ring of a telephone came from close by, startling me, and I glanced quickly over my shoulder. Down one hallway, just opposite an elevator and only a few feet past the last pillar, was an information counter. The woman who rapidly responded to the telephone was barely visible from where I stood. Just the clear, competent tones of her voice revealed her presence.

I crossed the reception area, and when she had routed the call at an old-fashioned switchboard and looked up at me expectantly, I smiled.

"Hello. I'm Rose Claypool. I'm looking for the office of the president, please."

The elderly woman didn't return my grin. She just bobbed a head of tightly curled gray hair and extended one long, pointy finger. "Down the hall, second door on the left. Right next to the bursar's office," she directed.

"Thank you." I set off at a rapid stride, squaring my shoulders and taking a few deep breaths. Soon my job would begin. In just a few moments I'd start a new phase in my life, which would hopefully be productive, fulfilling and—dare I think it?—permanent. A shudder of anticipation shot through me, and I gave my shoulders a shake to spend the nervous energy.

Pushing open the wooden door the receptionist had indicated, I entered the president's office. Wood-paneled, tastefully decorated, it looked like offices everywhere. Seated at a desk against one wall, the secretary looked up and gave me a businesslike smile of greeting.

"Ms. Claypool?" she inquired, consulting the appointment book before her.

"Yes. I have an appointment to see Dr. Brossman at nine-thirty." The clock in the room stood at exactly that, and I allowed myself a brief moment of congratulations on my timing.

A spasm of something like confusion flickered across the woman's plain features, wrinkling her brow and curling her lips. "Um," she said, stalling for time, her eyes darting to the door of the president's inner sanctum, then back to me.

"Yes?" I prodded when she fell into silence.

Her hand flipped the page of the appointment book back and forth, as if she were double-checking the date, making sure it was really September.

Shifting my weight from one pinched foot to the other, I waited.

"Dr. Brossman isn't in right now," she told me at last, and it was my turn to look puzzled.

"He *was* expecting me?" My voice betrayed the tiny flare of irritation I felt, and I joked to cover it up. "Did he oversleep? Get a flat tire?"

"I'm really not sure. You see, I'm just filling in for Dr. Brossman's usual secretary." She smiled and shrugged in apology.

"And that person obviously isn't here, either?" I shook my head in anticipation of her answer.

"No. Mrs. Vernon called in today. One of her sick headaches."

These headaches, I learned later, were legendary. Now I could feel one of my own coming on.

"Well, perhaps we can salvage this situation," I said, easing myself onto the corner of the desk and lifting one foot so I could waggle my toes. "The personnel committee of the college board hired me to be the new archivist, and this is my first day. I'll be putting all the historical files in order. Dr. Brossman was supposed to give me a hearty welcome to the job and then, I'd imagine, a tour of the place." I paused, heaved a gentle sigh, and went on. "I'm willing to skip the pep talk, but I would like a look around the school. To orient myself. Would someone be available to do that?"

"Um." Again her eyes roved the room. "Let me check for you, okay?" She bobbed up from behind the desk. "I'll be right back."

I could hear the click of her shoes as she started down the hall and hoped she wouldn't return with the little old lady from the information booth. Alone in the office, I deposited my coat on an empty chair and hung my umbrella from the arm. Then I took the opportunity to look around.

The walls held paintings of romanticized outdoor scenes, interspersed with framed articles about the college. A prominently displayed eight-by-ten glossy showed one heavyset man presenting a check to another equally overweight executive. Judging by the cut of their suits and the yellow of the newsprint, this was not a recent event. I leaned closer to read the caption:

Theodore Brossman, president of Lunham College, presents Councilman William Kimberly with a check for the proceeds from the school's Christmas-decoration campaign. Students at the school held a silent auction to raise money for the purchase of new Christmas ornaments to be used on downtown streetlights.

Straightening, I wondered. How old was the picture? What had the decorations looked like? Idle curiosity on my part, cut short by the return of the substitute secretary.

Wreathed in smiles now, she waved a hand, indicating the woman entering behind her. "I found someone!" she told me triumphantly. "This is Lily Thaler from Career Placement. She wasn't doing anything, so I asked her to show you around. Lily, this is Ms. Claypool."

Lily sent a withering glance at the back of the secretary's head before extending a hand to me. Her grip was firm and brief. "Hello. Pleased to meet you. Sorry you've gotten off to such a jumbled start here, but I'm afraid you'd better get used to it." Her voice was low and scratchy, like a smoker's, but it suited her. Short, with shoulder-length black hair and a compact figure, she struck me immediately as a no-frills person. I knew at a glance she was direct, not the type to mince words or sugarcoat unpleasant truths. I also knew we were going to get along.

"It's kind of you to take the time—" I began, but she cut me off.

"Let's get started, okay?" She pivoted on one heel, and I fell into step in her wake.

What started as a whirlwind tour on the first floor gradually slowed to a leisurely pace, allowing Lily and me plenty of time to get to know each other. She was a bit older than I, probably thirty-five or so, and had been at the school for six years. When I asked her if she liked working at Lunham, she shook her head.

"I'm taking the fifth on that one," Lily said, chuckling. "These walls have ears." She spread her arms to indicate the rather dreary brick lining the stairwell we'd just entered. "And I need this job." She added over her shoulder, "Let's just say each day brings a new adventure. The minute you clap your hand to your forehead and think to yourself, 'What next,' you find out."

This was not inspiring news for a newcomer, but then I knew every job had its drawbacks. Conspiracies, ill will, assorted feuds and friendships. In time, I'd learn them all.

Lily kept up a steady stream of conversation as we climbed the stairs to the second floor. I'd tuned out and was admiring the huge window on the landing. It must have measured eight feet square. Made up of different colored glass, it depicted an oak tree in the full bloom of summer. Behind the tree, a golden sun illuminated the scene.

If the sun were actually shining, I thought, hearing the persistent fall of rain outside, *this room would just glow!*

"What a gorgeous piece!" I exclaimed, breaking into Lily's sentence.

She was already on the second flight of stairs and looked down on me from a few feet above. "What? Oh, the window. Yes, it is lovely. Done by the art teacher. She does good work."

"The art teacher here?" I'd taken the window to be original to the building, which was nearly one hundred years old.

"Yes. Emily Welbourne. She's been here for ages. I think they built the place around her," Lily quipped. "But she's one of the sweetest people you'll ever meet. A true British gentlewoman, you know."

"Mm. I'd like to meet her." I followed Lily upward, reluctantly turning my back on the stained glass.

"She does all kinds of things," she told me. "Just about everything on display at the school is her work."

"Where is the art department? In this building?"

"Oh, yes. On the lower level, way at the north end of the building. The art gallery is in another wing," she clarified, "but the workrooms are here. This main building houses all the administrative offices and liberal-arts departments."

"Ah." I felt a pun coming on and made no effort to stop it. "The ad-lib building."

Lily gave a short, breathy laugh. "Very clever, Rose. I must remember that for the next tour I lead." Her tone was just a bit sarcastic, but the grin on her face told me she appreciated the humor.

Our tour continued with trips to the classrooms, testing center, science labs, library, and, as a finale, the archives.

To say I was underwhelmed at the sight of them would be an overstatement. The "archives" consisted of one room, shaped like an L, located directly next to the library. Quite obviously, it had previously been a storeroom and, judging by the pile of unlabeled boxes stacked over in a corner, still served in that capacity.

A bank of file cabinets must be where all Lunham College's historical treasures were stored. They ran the length of one wall, the long part of the L, from the doorway where I stood all the way to the window about twenty feet away. The walls were a dirty grayish color, and I decided my first order of business would be to get a fresh coat of paint on them.

My dismay must have shown on my face because Lily said, "As you can see, the archives have not been a priority in the past." She leaned against the doorjamb, arms folded, her head on an angle, watching me as I took a tentative step within.

"I knew this was a newly created position," I said, "but it looks as if no one has ever made *any* efforts to keep order here." I took a deep breath and blew a layer of dust off the top of a cabinet. "This is awful!"

Stacks of books and newspaper clippings were scattered about, the newsprint yellowed and curling at the edges. While I poked among what seemed at first glance to be mounds of unsorted debris, Lily gave me a little history lesson.

"The head librarian used to keep an eye on the historical files, but no one was ever really in charge. Then last spring one of the college's alumnae donated the money to pay your salary."

"Oh?"

"Yes. She was a history major here, and she's done quite well in business. Owns and operates a public-relations firm in Chicago now. Anyway, for some reason I can't quite imagine, she's always retained an active interest in Lunham. Made big yearly donations, bought computers for the main office. One year she sent a landscaping service in to plant flower beds on the campus!" Lily sounded incredulous, wondering why someone would spend hard-earned money on something as ephemeral as flowers.

"And now she's become interested in historical preservation?" I opened the drawers of a big wooden desk and found more jumble. Paper clips, rubber bands shriveled and dry, felt-tip markers with no caps, and bottles of dried-up correction fluid, which rattled like maracas when I shook them. I tipped the contents into the trash bin.

"Yes. She's provided a special fund from which the college is to pay for a full-time archivist. That's you. It's a wonderful gesture to make, and record keeping is certainly important."

"But—" I prodded. "There's a 'but' coming next?" Looking up from the trash, I caught her eye, and she smiled.

"Yes. Yes, there is. But there are plenty of people on campus who feel that money could have been put to better use on more immediate problems."

"Like what?"

"Like fixing up this place." Her hands went out in a gesture that encompassed not just one room but the whole college. "The heating system is deplorable. The roof leaks in more than one spot, and the electrical works are pretty outdated. Or, that woman could donate her public-relations expertise and help us raise funds for repairs, help us improve the college's image and attract more students. Enrollment has been slipping for the last several years. We're the only women's college left in this part of the state, you know, and, frankly, if the situation doesn't improve, there won't be a need for archivists or teachers, because this place will go under, just like all the others."

I turned my back on the mess of the room. There'd be plenty of time to get started after the tour. "I didn't realize the situation was so desperate," I said, snapping off the light.

Lily closed the door behind us, and we started down the main hall. "But don't let me paint too bleak a picture here," she continued. "Lunham's a good school. We get a superior rating in the college guidebooks."

"Yes, I know. I did a little research before accepting the job," I confessed.

"Oh." Her voice sounded flat, and I glanced at her quickly. She wrinkled her nose a bit and said almost sheepishly, "And I'm sure you heard all about that spot of trouble we had last month?"

Our footsteps slowed, our heels clicking in tandem along the quiet corridor. It was dim here, and I felt a damp chill in the air. I shivered, just a little.

"No." I drew out the word. Last month I'd been out West, visiting Mom and Dad. Arching my eyebrows, I invited a further explanation. "What happened?"

"Well, in a word"—she paused, clearly for dramatic effect—"murder!"

Chapter Two

"**M**urder!" The word popped out of my mouth, echoing Lily. "Here? Who was killed?"

Lily opened the door to another stairwell—how many were there in this place?—and we clattered down a level before she responded.

"A man was killed on property owned by the college. The campus is concentrated here around this building, but the property goes about a quarter of a mile all around. There's a woods behind us. The science classes go on expeditions there in the spring, cataloging plants and things. The art classes tramp out there too. It's a thick wood, but a well-traveled one."

"And, and?" I knew what woods were like. Trees, shrubs, plenty of birds. I wanted to hear about the crime.

"And that's where the body was found. In the woods. He'd been hit on the head with something heavy."

14

"Who was it? Was the killer caught?" I followed her down still more steps, watching the back of her head as it bobbed in front of me.

"Oh, the body was identified almost immediately. His name was Samuel Felber, and he was on the college's board of trustees. Owned the most prestigious art gallery in town. He was quite a pillar of society. Very active on the board too. Not like some of those lumps," she scoffed.

"Oh!" I gasped in surprise. "How awful!"

"Well, it was certainly a shock. And the most distressing part is, the killer hasn't been apprehended." We were at another door now. Before she pushed it open, Lily turned to me. "Frankly, I don't think the cops have a clue who did it. I'll bet we never find out who killed him or why."

"A real mystery," I added, appalled and intrigued. Would I have taken this job if I had known there might be a murderer loose? *Maybe*, I thought with brutal honesty. *There are fates worse than death.*

"I'd better explain where we're headed now," Lily broke into my thoughts. "We're in the basement. The building just north of here houses all the instructors' offices and, naturally, your office too. It's just a short walk outside, but since it's raining, we can take the tunnel."

"The tunnel?" Lunham College was becoming eerier by the moment.

Lily was expecting my reaction. Her laughter was sincere, and when she smiled, her eyes nearly disappeared. "I know. It's positively medieval," she agreed. "But, hey, here in the Midwest it sure comes in handy.

Snowing? Raining? Take the tunnel!" Her arms flung out, she gestured around us at a scene from a funhouse.

We'd come out in a tiny square room with a low ceiling consisting of big silver pipes—the inner workings of that antiquated heating system, I supposed. Set into each wall of the room was a door. They all looked identical, gray metal doors with no windows.

Pointing at each door in turn, Lily recited, "Amory Hall, that's teachers' offices. Whitnall Hall, the student dorm. And this one leads to the chapel."

"It's a good thing these are labeled," I said with a laugh. "Otherwise a person could get lost awfully easy!"

"It's still pretty easy," she confided, motioning for me to join her.

Our trip through the tunnel—more gray walls and pipes—was a short one. Up the steps on the other end, one left turn, and we faced a long corridor that stretched to the vanishing point, punctuated with doors like an apartment building.

"Your office is just here. Third door down."

As we approached, I could hear voices nearby. They sounded loud, but I figured that could be because the rest of the place had been so quiet.

With a bit of fanfare, Lily produced a key and handed it over. "Here you go. And, if you don't mind, I'll leave you to your own devices. I'm sure you'll be anxious to get settled in and do some exploring on your own." She glanced quickly at her watch. "I really should be getting back too."

"Oh, of course!" I hastened to assure her. "Thanks so much for the tour and the information. If I need to use the tunnel to get back, I'll leave a trail of bread crumbs."

"Good idea." She bobbed her head once, twice, and raised a hand in farewell. "We'll see you soon." Within seconds she'd vanished around the corner.

Left alone, I pushed the key into the lock and gave it a firm twist. The voices nearby had grown louder now, and I recognized the emotion they held as anger. Somewhere, very close at hand, someone was having a fight. I paused to listen, for no better reason than curiosity, but I couldn't make out any words.

Then, in a sudden burst, a deep voice shouted, "Fine! Have it your way! But let the consequences rest on your head!"

Before I could turn away or scoot inside my office, a door across the hall and down a bit flew open. An irate man, cheeks flushed red with fury, stepped out, slamming the door firmly behind him. Seeing me standing there, he favored me with a formidable glare, shifted the load of books tucked under his arm, and stalked off with heavy, thudding strides.

I blinked, stunned by the sheer energy generated by his rage. Whoever he was and whatever the argument had been, he was certainly in a lather.

Too bad, I thought. *I wonder what he looks like when he's not scowling.* As I watched, his figure grew smaller and smaller until he stopped at another door and jerked it open, giving it a rousing slam behind him.

One thing about this new job seemed certain. It wouldn't be dull.

An hour or so later the rumblings of my stomach reminded me lunchtime was near. A glance out the window into the rainy woods beyond confirmed the inclement weather. Should I follow the tunnel back to the cafeteria in the main building or sprint across the open lawn? In the end, I opted for the fifty-yard dash, welcoming the smell of fresh air and the cool mist on my cheeks. After retrieving my discarded trenchcoat and umbrella from the president's office, I followed my nose to the cafeteria on the lower level.

I loaded my tray with the usual assortment of cafeteria food—salad, some sort of noodle dish, and a chocolate-chip cookie for dessert—then scanned the vast, high-ceilinged room for the best table.

There was one beneath a window, looking out on the back lawn, that seemed promising. The sight of a discarded newspaper on one of the chairs clinched it. I headed rapidly in that direction.

My salad was limp, but the dressing was wonderful, and even the noodle casserole was tasty, I found as I nibbled away. The newspaper was spread on the tabletop beside my plate. I ate with my right hand, turned pages with my left, and worked my way through the international headlines to the local stuff.

All around me, the room filled up with students and instructors, their voices melding into one conversational roar. I managed to block it out for the most part, concentrating instead on the latest political blunders of state officials and plenty of small-town news. Plans to construct a shopping mall were creating a stir, taxes were up, and salaries were down. Ho hum.

One story in particular caught my eye, however, since it was such a reflection of a national concern. This midwestern region had been settled long ago by many Native American tribes, who had eventually lost their lands through treaties with the government. Now, it seemed, one local group was petitioning the historical society in town to return the artifacts on display to the tribes they originally came from.

The article was a lengthy one, interviewing the leader of the protest group, a man named Peter Moore. He made a good argument, and I found myself nodding in agreement as I read. At the top of the article was a picture taken at a recent demonstration outside the headquarters of the historical society. A group of people carrying signs and banners clustered on the steps of the building, listening intently while the leader gave what must have been a fiery address. His arm was raised, fist clenched, and his mouth was open in midsentence.

I bent over the page to get a closer look at him, then scanned the other faces. The group seemed to be a good cross section of society—men, women, young, old, black, white, and, of course, Native American, united by a belief. One face looked oddly familiar, and I blinked at the grainy black-and-white image, trying to place it. It was a man in his thirties, of average height, with dark hair grown a little too long on top. He wore heavy black glasses of an old-fashioned style, making him look very studious. Now, in a flash, I realized he looked just like that angry man in the hall.

I frowned, putting down my fork and reading the photo's caption. No one but the speaker was identified, and I decided to seek out Lily to get an answer. Who was this guy? What would have made him so angry? Something to do with this social dispute?

"Hmm," I muttered, reaching for my cookie and biting it absently. Even after I turned the page to the comics, he stayed in my mind, and only reading my horoscope drove him out.

You'll feel energized for new starts this week, I read. *It's time to put past concerns behind you and build for the future.*

I gave a chuckle and said under my breath, "I'm trying! I'm trying!"

I took the long way back to the office. I wanted to get a better look at the archives themselves. Maybe poke around a bit to get a sense of what condition the files were in, although I feared the worst.

At the door of the room, I paused. Just a few feet away, the huge library loomed, its great double doors open and inviting. On our tour, Lily and I had just peeked inside. Now I wanted a more lingering view.

Libraries have always been magic places for me. When I was growing up and my father was in the service, we'd moved around a lot. I'd lived in nine different places by the time I graduated from high school. All that shuffling made it difficult to have lasting friendships, but no matter where we were, books stayed good friends. They were always familiar and ready to share a good story. And the Dewey decimal system meant I could find my way around in just about every library. I could feel as if I belonged there, and that was quite a comfort when I was little. Truthfully, it's quite a comfort still.

I stepped into the foyer and felt the welcoming hush settle around me. Voices were subdued here and, far off, a typewriter clacked in broken staccato. The place had the wonderful smell of ink on paper, and I smiled to myself as I recalled the childhood joy of sniffing a brand-new book and running a loving hand over its cover.

If I weren't an archivist, I'd be a librarian, I thought, not for the first time.

All the public rooms at the college—auditorium, cafeteria, library—had high ceilings. The main room of the library was divided into an area for the card catalog, one for quiet study, and another featuring squashy sofas and wing chairs for small group discussions. The circulation desk, a big U-shaped affair, was directly inside the entrance, and beside this I spied what I was looking for—the book collection itself, housed in the stacks.

I wasn't the only person in the facility today, although business seemed slow. I chalked that up to the fact that the semester was just getting under way. The big research assignments would come later in the term, and then the place would become the hub of the campus.

A directory posted near a flight of metal spiral steps told me there were four floors of books and other materials; each floor was broken down into classification. When I put my hand on the smooth black railing and started upward, I had no particular goal in mind. At each landing I stepped off and spent some time browsing through the big, dark tiers. To conserve energy, no lights were on here, and I had to click switches on and off as I came and went down each aisle. By the time I reached the fourth floor, I knew what I wanted to see most—the view out the windows this high up.

I didn't bother turning on the lights as I headed to the far wall. The dim bit of daylight was enough to guide me. Beneath my feet old floor creaked and groaned, as if my steps were painful. I tried to tiptoe, but the noise continued. A row of study carrels made excellent nooks for reading, each one placed in front of a window. I chose one just off the main aisle and slid into the big wooden chair.

Propping my elbows up on the casement, I let my eyes roam the landscape stretched out before me. I could see a bit of the woods off to my left and wondered fleetingly just where that poor murdered man had been found. I didn't linger long on that topic. In the darkened, deserted quiet of the stacks, gothic ramblings were too easy an indulgence, and if I wasn't careful, I'd spook myself and end my visit with an undignified scramble down all those steps, back to civilization.

To the right, I recognized the long drive in from the highway. Past the road loomed the lake, stretching as far as my eyes could see. The water looked black from here, under a gray, overcast sky, just the thing for a vivid imagination. The window frame was cool under my fingers, and I pulled my hands away, shoving them deep into my pockets.

As I sat motionless, only the sound of my own breathing broke the silence. At first. Then I became aware of . . . something. I didn't really hear anything and, with my gaze fastened out the window, I didn't see anything, either. But gradually I could sense a presence close at hand.

The air around me thickened with tension, and I hunched my shoulders protectively, trying not to think about someone sneaking up behind me. The murderer, still at large, ready to seek another victim. Even as the thought was born, I tried to smother it.

Nonsense! the logical part of my brain shouted. *It's all in your head! No one is there. It's an old building. You're high up. It's the wind, of course. Just the wind. Why, if someone were walking up, the floor boards would let you know. You'd hear a very distinct—*

Creak.

Behind me, out of sight, but terrifyingly close, a foot trod on the noisy floor. It was an alarm that came too late because there was nowhere to go.

My eyes continued to look out the window, but I'd ceased any observation. I was frozen, like a deer in headlights, unable to move or react. The back of my neck tingled with fear, and I could feel a slight quaking in my legs. If I shrieked, would anyone hear me four floors down?

Clenching my hands into fists to quell their motion, I bit down hard on my lip to hold back that scream. Then, with a jolt of courageous bravado, I leaped up and whirled around, then staggered a few steps back.

"Did I startle you? Oh, I'm so sorry!"

I put my hand over my pounding heart and took a deep breath. "It's all right," I told the woman standing before me with a book in her hands. My smile was unsteady, I know, and I leaned against the heavy chairback for support.

My terror was on the far side of fifty. Tall and thin, she looked anything but frail, with a muscular build that contrasted sharply with her demure outfit. A bulky, obviously hand-knit cardigan in a dark shade of gray was tossed over her shoulders, and heavy, wire-rimmed glasses magnified her eyes to comical proportions. She wore tidy, charcoal-colored slacks. On her feet, I was surprised to see a pair of expensive running shoes, a bit grimy from use.

"I thought I was alone," I explained. "And then I heard a noise." I shrugged. "Well, I heard you." Making a helpless gesture, I grinned at my folly.

She failed to see any humor in the situation, drawing together pencil-thin brows that had been darkened to an unlikely shade of brown. They looked odd and rather severe when paired with her silvery hair.

"You're afraid of the library? There's nothing to be frightened of here, miss," she scolded, and I felt even worse.

"Yes, I realize that now. But I was looking at the woods and thinking about that dead man, and my imagination got the best of me."

At the mention of the murder, her face slammed shut. The frown left her brow. Her mouth set into a firm, unyielding line, and she registered no expression whatsoever. "I'm sure I don't know what you're talking about."

It seemed best to change the subject, and I hastily did so. Thrusting out my hand, I said, "I'm Rose Claypool, the new archivist."

She let my hand dangle there, just long enough to make me feel awkward, then gave it a brief touch. Her hand was cold. "My name is Harriet Easton," she told me. "I'm director of the library here at Lunham College."

I could tell from her triumphant tone she was proud of that title, and I wondered briefly if she did a good job in the role. It seems so often the wrong people are promoted and strut about, dropping fancy phrases, while all the real work is done by an underling. Up until now, in this new job, I'd been that underling. All too often for my taste.

"I didn't realize you'd arrived to start work," Harriet continued. "We all knew you were coming, of course. It was announced at the last staff meeting."

"Oh." I tried to express an interest. "That's nice."

She hurried on. "Have you seen the archives yet? They're just next door. I tidied up a bit in there for you."

My eyes widened. Tidied up! The place was a shambles! What had it looked like before? "Well, thank you so much," I told her sincerely. "It looks as if I have my work cut out for me. Has anyone ever made any effort to catalog the materials?" I asked. "They looked rather neglected to me."

Her thin, colorless lips compressed into a tight, unyielding line, and a spark came into her eyes, then quickly faded. She clenched her book tightly to her chest before answering. "Prior to your arrival, Ms. Claypool, the archives were officially untended. We're a small college, and you'll find we are all expected to wear many hats. In the interest of future generations—and on my own time—I have made humble attempts to organize the files over the years. I'm sure my efforts will not be up to your professional standards, but it was the best we could manage."

She paused for breath, then went on in a judgmental tone, "Of course, now that a handsome salary has been provided and an expert has been hired, I'm sure we can expect great things." Her nose elevated, and she looked down it at me, concluding, "I still think Lunham needs plenty of other material improvements more than it needs you."

I sighed, closing my eyes in a long, long blink. I was not getting off to a good start here at all. Dad always said I should think before I start talking. Score one for Dad.

Rather than try to salvage the situation, I extended an olive branch immediately. "I was just on my way over to the archives, Harriet. Perhaps, if you have time, you could come along. Show me what you've done." My voice rose at the end of the sentence, turning it into a question.

She was pleased, I could tell. A faint pink stained her cheek, and she fussed unnecessarily with her book. "I believe I could spare half an hour or so," she conceded, turning to lead the way down the stairs.

As we clattered in an endless spiral, she chatted in a reserved but conversational tone, as if we were at a cocktail party making small talk. *Aha,* I thought, giving myself a mental clap on the back for my clever deduction. *Harriet is one of those folks who need constant attention. She expects a deferential attitude. Ego coddling from her subordinates.*

If a groan escaped my lips at this point, I'd put it down to my breathless state, caused by descending the stairs. It wasn't a groan of dismay or annoyance. Oh, no. Definitely not.

Harriet stayed for closer to two hours that day. Her tour of the archives was lengthy and detailed. There was a bit of organization, I found, beneath the unsorted piles of material. Harriet brushed off the jumbled state of the room, telling me, quite rightly, that that was my problem now.

I was glad when she finally excused herself and closed the door quickly behind her. When I glanced at the clock and realized it was already late afternoon, I decided to knock off early. If I left now, I reasoned, looking once more at those horrid dirty walls, I could make a stop at the local hardware store and get some supplies. Harriet had said we were expected to wear many hats. Tomorrow I'd be the cleaning lady.

Chapter Three

"**R**ose! Hey, Rose! Wait up!"

I stopped in the middle of the hallway, secretly grateful for the chance to set down the heavy paint cans I carried in each hand. Stretching up tall, I clenched my hands to relieve the strain from the cans' wire handles and watched Lily approach.

She wore a very professional-looking suit this morning, in a gorgeous shade of gold, with a patterned blouse underneath done up in every autumn color. I felt like a poor relation in my painting duds, faded jeans and an old sweater.

"Hi, Lily." My smile was genuine. "What's up?"

She came to a stop beside me and looked me over, up and down. "I think I should be asking you that. What are you doing?"

"I would have thought it was obvious," I kidded. "I'm going to paint the archives."

"But you can't do that!" she told me, her dark eyes wide with disbelief. She jerked her hand up, studied her watch, and announced, "The staff meeting starts in ten minutes." Her words hung there, stark and unavoidable. From the anxious look on her face, I knew she wasn't joking.

"What? You never mentioned any meeting yesterday," I sputtered. "Should I have known about this?"

Lily's eyes drifted off over my shoulder as she thought. "I might have forgotten to tell you," she admitted. "The notice was posted in the staff lounge, though."

"But I never saw it!" My voice rose, tinged with horror at my realization of the impending scene. I would meet my coworkers—and the college president—in my painting clothes. "Oh, no," I groaned, slumping.

"It will be all right," Lily attempted to console me, patting my arm as if I were a child. Her tone wasn't very convincing, though, and I grimaced as she hurried on. "This could work out to your benefit. Everyone will see at a glance what an industrious person you are. Eager to get to work. Willing to take on dirty tasks. A real take-charge kind of gal." She made a rousing motion, swinging her fist like a cheerleader after a touchdown.

"Sure," I agreed, not making any attempt to hide my sarcasm. "Why, I should have planned it this way. What a marvelous scheme!" Peeling off my head scarf, I ran a hand through my hair in agitation.

"Oh, relax. Nobody will even notice. These meetings are so deadly dull, some folks sleep straight through them, I swear. C'mon. We'd better hurry. It wouldn't do to be late besides." She hoisted one can, I took the other, and we set off down the hallway.

*   *   *

Lily pushed open the door of the conference room, and I followed her inside. We'd dropped the paint cans in her office, so I was spared at least one indignity. Looking around the room, I realized I'd been spared another. We were the first to arrive.

"Where is everyone?" I asked.

Lily shrugged. "We don't like these meetings much. Everyone races in at the last possible second. Or later." She took a seat in the far corner of the second-to-last row of chairs, motioning me to sit behind her. With a bank of windows on one side, the rear wall behind me, and Lily directly in front, I'd be pretty much blocked from view. I sank into my place just as the door opened and others began to arrive.

Within a few minutes the meeting room was two-thirds full. Many people smiled in my direction, including me in their greeting for Lily. When the president of the college arrived, all small talk ended, and it was eyes front.

I would have known he was the person in charge even if I hadn't recognized him from his portrait in the main hallway. He had the air of blustery authority some folks get. His confident strut and purposeful stride brought him rapidly to the podium at the front of the room, and he favored us all with a benevolent, if patronizing, smile.

"Good morning, all," he intoned, raising beefy palms to the sky like a holy man delivering a blessing. Dr. Brossman was a big man. Six feet tall, I guessed, and easily two hundred and fifty pounds. His gray hair and chubby cheeks emphasized his resemblance to everyone's grandfather. I wondered how old he was. The newspaper photograph I'd seen in his office showed a younger man. Darker hair, smaller potbelly.

He tapped some papers against the edge of the lectern, as if gathering his thoughts. Then, taking a deep breath, he launched the meeting.

I've never been one for meetings. I find them singularly unproductive. Two or three people always seem to run the whole show while the rest of us take notes and daydream. This one was no different.

From my vantage point at the back of the room, I could see staff members scratching into their notebooks with pens or pencils, but, more often than not, their labors appeared to be doodles.

Two rows in front of me and over one seat, the angry young man from yesterday sat. His pencil flew quickly across the paper in front of him, darting here and there in a seemingly random fashion. As I watched, a face began to emerge on the page, and I had to stifle a laugh when I recognized the caricature of Dr. Brossman. The artist had exaggerated the potbelly and the double chin and captured the man in mid-bluster, mouth open, pontificating.

He must have heard my aborted chuckle because he turned his head, ever so slightly, glancing over his shoulder at me. The heavy framed glasses he wore contained thick lenses, and the glare of the lights bouncing off them prevented me from seeing his eyes. One dark eyebrow was lifted, however, in a way best described as sardonic.

I looked pointedly from his face to the drawing and back again, then tilted my head to silently indicate my admiration. He didn't smile, not even a little, but lifted his shoulders in a shrug of dismissal.

When he was facing forward again, I tapped Lily on the shoulder and borrowed her notebook just long enough to write, *Who is that guy with the Clark Kent specs?* I passed it back and waited while she dashed off a reply.

Duncan Pearce. History professor. Tell you later.

The president had moved on by this time, past humdrum financial matters, and was now into departmental reports. Each department head was called upon in turn to give a brief description of current activities. Being new to the organization, I appreciated this, since it gave me a good introduction to who was who and what plans and procedures were taking place.

Some departments had nothing to report, while others droned on in great detail. Harriet, the librarian, was received with heavy sighs and much fidgeting. It didn't take long to see why. Her presentation, delivered in a slumber-inducing monotone, lasted a full fifteen minutes.

I watched Duncan's paper carefully, waiting for his pen to jump into action and deliver another lethal caricature. But he'd removed a sheaf of papers from the briefcase at his feet and was absorbed in leafing through them.

At last, after a prompt from Dr. Brossman, Harriet wound it up and resumed her seat. Duncan's turn came next. He gave his glasses a firm push up the slope of his nose, cleared his throat, and began.

"As you are all well aware, this year marks the centenary of Lunham College. This is an historical event and, as such, deserves public recognition. To this end, plans are under way for a full-scale celebration, beginning with the widespread distribution of pamphlets highlighting the college's achievements and in-house historical displays that will be open to the public." He glanced down at the papers he held, turned to the next one, and continued. "The alumnae association will be coordinating a formal dinner dance as the wrap-up event. This will also serve as a much-needed fund-raiser."

He went on to enumerate the specifics of the festivities and, while part of my mind listened with interest, the other part examined the man himself.

This was the first time I'd been able to get a good look at him, and I took my time. His dark hair grew low to a widow's peak, brushed back to keep the length from his eyes. Cut short on the sides, it was longer again at the back, curling over the frayed edge of his collar. The stubble of beard cast a shadow across his cheeks and chin but couldn't hide the dimple that creased as he spoke. I put him at about thirty-four, judging by the fine lines just beginning to appear at the corners of his eyes. He was trim, although the well-worn tweed blazer and baggy corduroys he wore did little to show off an athletic frame.

I tuned into the discussion again when I heard my name spoken.

"When the new archivist, Rose Claypool, arrives, I'll be consulting her for help gathering materials from the historical files."

I sat up straighter as his eyes swept the room.

"She's here now," the president offered. "Arrived

yesterday, I believe." Since he hadn't met me, he too searched the crowd of faces for the one that would be unfamiliar.

There was no avoiding it. I raised my hand. "I'm Rose Claypool." As all heads swiveled my way, I remained rooted to my chair and gave a friendly little wave. "Hello, everyone."

"Stand up, stand up," Dr. Brossman ordered. "The folks at the front can't see way back there."

I put my hand on the back of Lily's chair—it was shaking from her silent laughter—and rose to my feet. I'm tall—five feet ten—so when I stood, I was visible, all right. Old sweater, old jeans, no makeup.

Duncan scowled, although from appearances he certainly didn't seem qualified to be a critic. The president frowned, and a few other looks of disapproval were apparent.

"I'm going to be painting a few walls today," I hurried to explain. "Any volunteers would certainly be welcome."

That remark did the trick. Everyone instantly looked away, across the room, into their laps, anywhere but at me.

I smiled and sat down.

After the meeting all the staff members milled around, forming little clusters of conversation, all buzzing with excitement over Dr. Brossman's final announcement.

The good doctor seemed to have quite a flair for the dramatic, and he'd offered proof positive of the fact at the end of the meeting.

"I've saved the best news for last," he'd told us,

beaming from ear to ear. "In conjunction with the centenary celebrations, we've already received our very first donation."

The crowd waited expectantly, silence ringing in the air. All doodling had stopped among the staff now.

"The O'Brien family, who are known throughout this community for their charitable donations, have turned their attentions to Lunham College. They have graciously presented us with a very valuable antique." Here, his smile wavered ever so slightly before he concluded. "A rare seventeenth-century illuminated Bible has been given to the school."

He consulted some notes on the lectern as everyone in the room reacted with looks of astonishment or appreciation. A few whispered comments to one another, their voices just a hiss in the big room.

"It, um. . . . It is especially unique, or so they tell me, because it is accompanied by a bookmark encrusted with gemstones." He looked up and gestured as he described it. "It's a silk ribbon, backed with leather or something, and the jewels are in the pattern of a stained-glass window from a thirteenth-century cathedral in France."

He lifted his heavy shoulders, grinning at his stunned audience. "There will be an official presentation ceremony within a few weeks, and then the Bible will be placed in a glass cabinet in the school chapel."

"The chapel?" Harriet's voice grated on the ear as she snapped out the question. "An item like that belongs in the library, of course. A valuable book should be displayed near other books. I suggest we put it near the old globe, under the map of the world on the east wall."

"Well, thank you so much for your thoughts, Harriet,

but I'm afraid the O'Brien family was quite adamant on this point. The Bible will be stored in the chapel, as they request."

"But—" Harriet was ready for a debate.

Dr. Brossman was faster. "All the details will be passed along as they become available. I would like to see as many of you as possible at the presentation ceremony. But, of course, attendance isn't mandatory. Meeting adjourned." If he'd had a gavel, he'd have slammed it down with a resounding thump. Instead, he wheeled about and marched firmly for the door, exiting quickly. Harriet followed on his heels, and I wondered if he'd managed to dodge her in the hallway.

Lily stood up, arching her back and letting out a long sigh. "What do you think of that?" she asked, one hand rubbing at the small of her back. "I'd have thought an historical item should be placed in the archives. Your department."

I shook my head. "I'm not about to get embroiled in controversy my first week on the job. I think all viewpoints have merit, but that doesn't mean much if these O'Briens are dead set on having the Bible in the chapel."

"Yes." Lily's breath came out on a sigh. "You certainly don't tell the O'Briens what to do with their own money. Half this town is named after them, you know, and I suppose we should be grateful. Still, it seems these gifts always have strings attached."

"Not only that," Duncan Pearce said, sidling up between us, "but with all their money and our desperate financial state, a gift of cold, hard cash would have been more appropriate."

Lily nodded. I didn't say anything at all.

Duncan regarded me sternly, looked me smack in the eye, and said, "I suppose you think that sounds odd. Traitorous. A history professor frowning on a gift of historical importance."

"No, no," I hedged. Actually, I hadn't been thinking about that at all. I might have, in time, but the thought hadn't even crossed my mind yet.

"Once you're here a bit longer, you'll see what I mean," he told me. "Lunham is not in fantastic fiscal health."

"So I've heard." It seemed the formalities had been neglected long enough, so I thrust out my hand, smiled, and said, "Let's make this official. I'm Rose Claypool."

His eyes darted down to my hand, and his own came out automatically. "Duncan Pearce, history department." His hand touched mine, warm and firm, and my smile froze on my face.

After a moment I cleared my throat. "I'm looking forward to hearing about your plans for the centenary displays," I told him sincerely. "Obviously, I haven't had much opportunity to see what's in the files yet, but perhaps we could meet soon and discuss your ideas. That way, as I organize, I can keep an eye out for specific items."

He nodded, then swept a hand up and through the long locks on his forehead. "Certainly. Certainly. Do you have your calendar handy? We could set up a tentative time right now."

I looked down at my casual attire and shoved my hands into the pockets of my jeans. "I, um, didn't exactly come prepared," I said, glancing at Lily. "I wasn't aware a meeting was scheduled."

Lily, catching my look, just shrugged and grinned.

"Oh, well, another time then. I'll know where to find you."

We all took a few steps closer to the door. The pockets of conversation were breaking up now, people wandering toward the exit at a leisurely pace. Once we were out in the hall, we stopped. Lily and I would be heading back to her office for my paint cans. Duncan showed every sign of tagging along. He'd kept up a steady stream of chitchat with Lily as we ambled out the door, saying things that struck her funny. Her low, booming laughter filled the air, echoing in my ear and drawing glances from others nearby.

Now, in the hall, Lily told him our errand. "Duncan, put those muscles to work," she said, reaching out to playfully squeeze his biceps. "Come and carry some paint cans for Rose." She tipped her head at me.

"Oh, that's not necessary," I felt bound to protest. "They aren't that heavy, and there are only two—"

"No, no," Duncan cut me off. He smiled at me, and it's a sight I'll always remember. One corner of his mouth went up higher than the other, making him look boyish and just a bit hesitant. His eyes were green. Green and gold and full of sparks. "Let me help."

Ten minutes later Duncan and I were walking toward the archives, each of us carrying a paint can. We'd had a brief discussion on the color—a warm shade of mauve—debating its merits, or lack thereof.

"Pink?" he'd questioned, examining the label.

"Hardly that," I'd retorted, picking up on his teasing tone. It was just like the voice he'd used when speaking to Lily. Friendly, gently chiding. "It's called mauve. It'll make the room cozy and user-friendly. Warm. Inviting."

"It will make it look like a family restaurant," he'd responded with a shake of his head. "Those are always mauve and gray, with brass lamps. Better not add any brass lamps, or I'll want to order breakfast every time I walk into the room."

I laughed at that, imagining the scene. At the door I fumbled in my pocket for my key and snapped on the overhead light. The fluorescent bulbs flickered to life, illuminating the cramped and jumbled room.

Duncan set his can down and let out a long, low whistle. He put his hands on his hips and turned in a slow circle, surveying the wreckage. "You know, I've only been in here once or twice. I didn't realize how far gone it was."

I let my own can thump onto a clear spot on the desk. "It's been neglected, that's for sure. But I'm sure it can be salvaged. Some tender, loving care, a little elbow grease. It'll be okay." I spoke with confidence, optimistic.

"A *lot* of elbow grease," he corrected me. "I don't envy you the job."

"Well, that's because you aren't the archivist." I moved around the room, picking up boxes from the floor and putting them onto tabletops. "If you were, you'd see this as a treasure hunt. A maze to be followed straight through to the end."

"And the pot of gold?"

I straightened up, let another box crash onto the table, and grinned. "Exactly." When we looked at each other,

I knew he understood perfectly. His answering smile connected with mine, and I felt that odd sensation of mutual attraction. That toasty feeling in the pit of my stomach rapidly radiated in both directions, tingly up my arms and down to my toes. There was no way I was going to get romantically involved now. Not with Duncan, not with anyone. Knowing this, I relaxed and allowed myself to enjoy the moment.

"I'd, um, I'd stay and help you, but I've got to get ready for my class this afternoon." He sounded genuinely dismayed.

I waved his concern away. "Thanks for the offer, Duncan, but I don't need any help. I've painted plenty of rooms in my lifetime." I gave my eyes a roll. "Believe me!"

"Oh, well, in that case. . . ." He flapped a hand in casual farewell. "I'll see ya."

I waved. "See ya." Reaching into my back pocket, I extracted the can opener I'd brought along and popped the top off the first can of paint. The chemical smell of the stuff wafted instantly upward. Dipping in a long wooden stick, I stirred the mixture, looking up to watch Duncan's disappearing form.

As I set to work, I wished I'd had the foresight to bring a radio. A little racket to break the silence would have been welcome.

I had completed all of one wall and had just begun on the second when a light rap sounded on my door. Without looking up, I called out, "Come on in!" I loaded the paint roller, set it against the wall with a squish, and looked over my shoulder to see who my visitor was.

The tiny woman standing in the doorway said, "Hello," bobbing a head of reddish hair. In her youth that hair must have gleamed like a ruby, a rich, dark, red. Now, in old age, it was faded and liberally mixed with white. "I didn't get a chance to greet you this morning at the meeting," she told me as she advanced into the room. Her voice was gently accented with the tones of her native England. "I'm Emily Welbourne, the head of the art department."

Setting down my roller, I wiped my hands on a rag and extended one. "I'm pleased to meet you. I'm Rose."

"Yes, yes, I know." She smiled, reminding me of the Queen Mum as her round cheeks fell into fine lines. Since she was standing just a few feet from me, the scent of her lavender perfume was evident. "Welcome to Lunham College," she added, looking around the room.

It looked even worse than before just then. All the file cabinets were pulled away from the walls. Any other furnishings were gathered together in the middle of the room.

"Oh, dear." She sighed. "What a way to start your new job! You must think it awful of us to let the place go like this." Emily turned slowly, one hand resting on her cheek.

I shrugged. It didn't really matter what I thought. I had a job to do, and I was looking forward to doing it—although I wasn't looking forward to all the painting still ahead. "It's a challenge, that's for sure," I told her. I pushed my hands against the small of my back, where an ache was already beginning.

"You know what would look nice in this room? A mural. Just above the file cabinets. A mural of the school and the grounds as they would have been one hundred years ago." Emily had gotten a dreamy look in her eyes and was staring at the wall in question, arms up, hands spread, framing the view.

I blinked in wonder, drawn by the suggestion. "That would be wonderful," I agreed. "So appropriate. So special." I hesitated. "Are you, um, volunteering for the job?"

"I'm pretty busy right now with some projects for the centennial, but I'd bet I could squeeze it in. I have a few very talented students who could lend a hand. Let me see if I can recruit them." She smiled at me with confidence, and I knew she was that rare sort of instructor who could get students to move mountains. Just because she liked them, just because they liked her and they genuinely enjoyed working together.

"Oh, that would be marvelous!" I said. "Maybe I can even help out a little. I draw a bit," I added shyly.

This was the woman responsible for that glorious window in the stairwell and all those other banners and statues I'd seen lining the corridors of the school. My rudimentary skills paled in comparison to her talents, and I knew it.

"Do you now? Well then, we'll put you to work as well. Perhaps you'd be interested in my sketching class. Wednesday evenings, in the art department. A few of us—staff, students, and friends—get together for an hour or two. It's just for fun. No grading or judging. What do you think?"

I nodded. "I think I'd like that. What time?"

"Seven o'clock. We usually work until nine. Sometimes we go out for tea—well, coffee—afterward. It will give you a chance to get to know some of the others."

"That should be fun. Do I bring my own supplies?"

"No, no. We'll provide all that." Emily took a last look around. "I suppose I shouldn't keep you from your work. And I do have plenty of my own as well." She laughed, in a clear, high sound like a bell ringing. "Toodle-oo!"

After she'd gone, it was quieter than ever, although my thoughts kept me busy enough. I pondered the mural, the O'Briens' precious gift, the murdered man no one seemed anxious to discuss. The painting went rapidly then, my arms moving automatically, as if I were a robot, repeating the same motion over and over again in a mind-numbing pattern.

I took a break for lunch, eating alone at a corner table since the few people I'd met were nowhere in sight. Anyone looking at me would have thought I was a student, judging by appearances. Or a custodian's assistant, perhaps, if they looked close enough to see the paint on my nose.

At the end of the long day, I felt a great sense of accomplishment. The room, while still unorganized, was now tinted a warm, welcoming shade. Just looking at it improved my spirits, and I smiled as I stood back to view the results of my labors.

My step was light as I left the room, carefully locking it behind me. Daylight was just beginning to fade, so I took the outdoor path to the teachers' office building. I wanted to do a bit of unpacking and had dropped off a box of reference books and materials in my office first thing that morning.

I'd just swung open the outer door of the building when a voice I recognized shouted, "Hey, wait up! Hold the door!"

I leaned against the open door and waited.

Duncan loped across the lawn from the parking area behind the building, bending under the weight of a cumbersome cardboard box. "Thanks," he puffed as he approached. "I was wondering how I'd maneuver all this." He moved past me into the hall, and I let the door close behind us.

"What is all that?" I pointed at the box.

"Civil War memorabilia. For a class I'm doing on American history. I've found the use of visual aids can make all the difference between delivering a monologue to a room of bored faces and having a lively discussion with plenty of student participation." He chuckled, making that lopsided smile dance across his features.

"Is all this yours?" I gestured at the heavy box as we went past my office door and continued down the corridor to his.

Duncan crinkled his nose in an effort to inch his glasses up from where they drooped. "Oh, yes. It's my thing—the Civil War."

"Hmm. Do you belong to one of those societies that reenact the battles and all?"

"Not yet, but I probably will someday soon."

We stopped at his door, and he gestured to his jacket pocket, bobbing his head to the left. "Could you get my keys, do you think?"

I felt self-conscious, putting my hand into his pocket, feeling the warmth of it so close to his body. It didn't take long to locate the key ring. I pulled it out and held it aloft.

"The gold one, with the holes in it."

It fit smoothly in the lock, and I pushed open the door, reaching for the light switch at the same instant.

Duncan let the box drop onto the uncluttered surface of his desk. "So, how goes the painting?"

I grinned. "Fine, thanks. It makes such a difference. You'd be amazed."

He nodded. "I'll bet." Rubbing his hands together, he went on. "I was just about to go get some dinner. Would you care to join me?"

I hesitated before responding. I liked Duncan. He was friendly, interesting, even intriguing. It was the intriguing bit that decided me. Looking at him, I recalled the picture of the protest rally on behalf of the Native American artifacts. He'd been right there, in the middle of things, taking a stand. Why? I wondered.

"Yes," I said. "I'd like that."

His eyebrows arched just a bit, as if he were surprised at my acceptance. "Great! Let's take my car."

His car, I soon found, was the most run-down one in the lot. It was old, shaped like a box, and painted a startling shade of yellow where the rust hadn't poked through. The back bumper was a montage of stickers for worthy causes—whales, political prisoners, solar energy.

"You know," I said, pointing at the stickers, "I would have guessed this was your car. It suits you."

Duncan paused in the motion of opening the door. "I'm not sure I like the sound of that. Would you care to elaborate?"

I moved past him onto a cracked vinyl seat, poking the stuffing back in with my finger. "Well, I just mean I can't picture you in a red Ferrari or anything so ostentatious."

Licking his lips, he said, "Don't be fooled. I'd love a Ferrari. But I can only afford this."

I saw the corner of his mouth turned up in a look of definite amusement. "My mistake then," I ventured. "Appearances are deceiving."

He laughed, nodding, sending the long locks on the top of his head waving in rhythm. "Something to remember about this place, Rose."

There didn't seem to be any appropriate response to that remark, so I said nothing, turning my attention out the window to the scenic view of the lake slipping by.

Chapter Four

Ten minutes later we were in the heart of the business district. In the older part of town, it was made up of family-operated stores, interspersed with newer enterprises like video shops and ethnic restaurants.

"Where are we headed?" I asked as Duncan expertly parallel-parked in front of a furniture store proudly labeled, *Serving the community since 1902.*

"Here." He pointed at what appeared to be a little hole-in-the-wall diner.

I'd been worried about my attire, still dressed in my painting clothes, but the sight of the lighted beer sign in the window put me at ease. When I saw the nameplate over the door, I felt even better.

"The Oasis," I read aloud, looking to Duncan.

"Middle Eastern food," he told me. "Have you ever tried it?"

I quickened my step as he joined me on the sidewalk. "Are you kidding? It's my favorite!" Suddenly I realized I was starving. Lunch had been a very

long time ago, and my stomach rumbled in anticipation. I grabbed onto his elbow and gave a little
tug.

The interior of the restaurant was a surprise. It wasn't
tiny at all, but stretched back quite far. The decorations weren't quite suited to the menu. Dark paneling,
red-leather booths, and checkered tablecloths made it
obvious the place had been Italian in an earlier incarna-
tion. A few papyrus paintings had been hung at random
intervals, and some Egyptian-inspired brass plates tried
to convey the proper atmosphere.

"Best pita bread in town," Duncan assured me as the
host seated us at a table against the wall.

Nodding, I picked up the menu and flipped it open.
"Falafel? Tabouli? Hummus? They've got everything!"

"Say, you sound like an old pro. It took me months to
learn those pronunciations, and I still have trouble with
baba . . . baba. . . ." He fumbled with the word.

"Babaghannouj," I said glibly, pointing my nose in
the air. "It's eggplant and tahini, basically."

"It's delicious, that's all I know," Duncan said,
laughing.

We placed our order, and when the waiter had gone,
Duncan asked, "How come you're so familiar with the
lingo here?"

That answer was easy. "I lived in the Middle East, of
course."

"Really?"

"Yes, really." I shrugged. "But then, I've lived just
about everywhere. My father was in the service."

"Oh, an Army brat." He smiled when he used the
phrase, but I scowled nonetheless.

"Don't, please." I held up my hand. "I wasn't a brat. I hate that phrase. It's followed me my entire life." I know I sounded tired and a little crochety, but I couldn't help that. If there were two words I never wanted to hear again in my life, those were the ones. *Army brat.* I shuddered.

"Oops, sorry. I didn't know." Duncan broke off lamely, and I felt sorry for causing the awkward moment.

The waiter arrived with soup—hot, steamy lentil laced with carrots—and the legendary pita bread.

Once he'd gone, I apologized. "You had no way to know I detest that term. But now you do, so. . . ." I took the slice of bread Duncan offered me and shredded it into my soup bowl, leaving my threat dangling in the air between us.

"Don't worry. I'll never use it again," he assured me. "Where else was your dad stationed?"

I sipped my soup, poking the bread beneath the surface with my spoon. "Europe. Japan. Canada. A few different states." Other people always seemed impressed by my litany of locations. I could never understand why. I didn't choose to travel. I never asked for a nomadic childhood. Wouldn't recommend one, either. Still, most people were awed and told me I was lucky. I looked across the table to Duncan, waiting.

He said, "That must have been awful." His sincerity was clear in his voice, deep and steady. His expression was solemn, and he'd set down his spoon.

I laid mine down as well and leaned toward him on my elbows. The light in the corner was dim and cozy, but I could see his eyes. "Yes," I said in a voice like a whisper. "It was. Maybe some people can live like that.

Maybe some even thrive on it. Not me, though. I hated it. All of it."

Duncan's arm stretched out across the table, and his hand settled gently over mine in a reassuring, comforting gesture. I looked down, noting the fine dark hairs that peppered his hand, the smooth square nails, a scar at the base of one finger.

"It's over now, Rose. You can stay here at Lunham College forever, if you like. You don't ever have to travel again, unless it's by choice. You're a grown-up now."

All the words I'd said to myself over and over. How many times? Too many times.

"You'd think so, wouldn't you?" I laughed, sliding my hand out from under his. "This is really great soup!" My change of subject was clumsy and obvious.

Duncan blinked, accepting the abrupt transition without question. "Yes. They tell me it's a secret mixture of spices," he said.

We ate in silence for the time it took to empty our bowls. The waiter appeared with our entrees, and as I cut into a falafel patty stuffed with pine nuts, I asked Duncan about his childhood.

"Oh, pretty unremarkable, I'm afraid." He lifted his shoulders in a shrug of dismissal. "I'm the oldest of four, born and raised about twenty miles from here. Dad was a cop. Mom stayed at home and took care of us." His face clouded, and he looked away as he went on. "Dad was killed ten years ago, during a robbery. The robber was caught. He's sitting in a jail cell now, and my father is dead and my mom is alone." The anger and resentment he still felt was clear in his voice. His lips were pressed together tight, and his hand had clenched around his fork. "I try to get over to see Mom a couple times a week. And my brothers are really good that way too."

I nodded. It was obvious he felt a great deal for his mother. Missed his father a lot too. If his siblings felt that way, they'd be united by caring and concern.

He spoke again before I could comment. "They—my brothers—are all married, so they bring the grandkids along, and Mom likes that." A gentle smile touched his lips. "They're good kids. Cute and charming and smart."

"It's just a lucky thing you're so unbiased," I teased him, reaching for my water glass.

I was rewarded with another lopsided smile as he said sheepishly, "Well, I am a proud uncle, I guess."

"I guess," I echoed, and we laughed together.

He turned serious again, back into a college professor. "Living in all those different spots must have taught you an awful lot about getting along with people. Living in different cultures, I mean."

I took another bite as I nodded. "Yes, definitely. I learned to make friends quickly. But I also learned to never get too close. When you know you won't be around long, it doesn't pay to get your emotions entangled with someone you'll have to leave behind. I learned to be tolerant, too, of the differences in people and the way they live."

It was his turn to nod, and I saw an opening for a question of my own. "You understand others. You care about other cultures, right?"

"Hmm?" He frowned, his eyebrows nearly meeting above his eyes.

I dipped a slice of pita bread into rich, creamy hummus dip and then gobbled it up. Then, I confessed, "I saw your picture in the paper, Duncan. At the Native American protest."

"Oh!" The light of understanding came on in his eyes. "Yes. It was an interesting event. I find the issue quite thought-provoking. And not just because of the historical perspective." As the waiter came in our vicinity, Duncan flagged him down and ordered coffee for us both.

Our meal passed quickly after that. Duncan went to great lengths to explain his concerns about what he termed "wrongful use of artifacts."

"There comes a point," he told me, stirring sugar into his coffee, "where history and compassion must take separate paths. Something may have historical significance—a skeleton or an article of ceremonial clothing—but its personal significance may be greater. Would you hand over an antique christening gown? One that's been in the family for generations?"

I thought on the topic, holding my coffee cup with both hands. "Perhaps," I told him at last. "But if I did, it would be my choice. A voluntary gesture."

"Exactly." Duncan nodded, and I saw his glasses inch down his nose with the motion. In the reflected light from overhead, the lenses looked extra thick and heavy.

He must have terrible eyesight, I thought, my mind wandering. *He should get those new thin lenses. The plastic ones.* I made a note to mention it and turned my attention back to his conversation.

"That's the issue, to me. Choice. We all need to preserve our past and learn from it. We need places to store these treasures and make them readily available. Museums!" He held out a hand to emphasize the concept. "But we must always, always, safeguard our sense of humanity. Make certain we realize that relics are not inanimate objects dropped from the sky. They are embodied with memory, with the collective past, with real lives of real people."

I nodded. As an archivist, I knew only too well how easy it could be to get excited over a special find and want it for a collection, momentarily forgetting its value to the owner. To me, a photo may illustrate a perfect example of turn-of-the-century style and design. To someone else, it's a photo of Great-Uncle Gottlieb, a much more special relationship.

"Well, just for the record"—I reached for the last slice of bread, offering half of it across the table to Duncan—"I think you're right, and I think the Native Americans are right. You set a good example for your students by being politically active. It'll help teach them to be responsible citizens."

Duncan gave a snort and laughed, showing white teeth and plenty of them. "I wish the college viewed things your way. Dr. Brossman called me in for a little chat after that picture ran. Told me he'd prefer not to see anything like that again."

"Like what?"

Duncan shrugged. "I suppose he considers it bad publicity, associating with a controversial topic. And, of course"—his voice took on a sarcastic tone, and he wagged a finger in my direction—"we certainly can't afford negative press. Not during our centennial and especially not after that unpleasantness last month."

"Unpleasantness? Oh, yes! The murder!" I didn't want to appear ghoulish in my eagerness for detail, so I aimed for a casual tone. "Lily just mentioned that briefly my first day here, and I haven't had a chance to ask for more details. Would you tell me?" I asked. "I'm just curious, and if the murderer hasn't been caught, it could be important to know the whole story."

"Well, I don't really know the whole story, but I'll gladly give you all the scuttlebutt."

The waiter refilled our coffee cups, and we ordered dessert. I picked carefully at a heavenly pistachio pastry as Duncan began.

"The . . . incident took place last month, just after that rainy week. The police were hoping for footprints in the mud near the body, but there were so many footprints, any clues were lost."

I arched an eyebrow, and he explained. "Too many onlookers—police and otherwise. Plus the prints of whoever found the body."

I nodded. "Of course. Go on."

"The victim was Samuel Felber, president of the college's board of directors. He'd been hit with a blunt instrument on the back of the head. Did him in pretty quickly."

"Was he killed in the woods, where he was found?"

Duncan regarded me thoughtfully as he used his fork to cut the dessert. "Y-yes," he said slowly, lifting the fork to his mouth. As he chewed, his eyes never left my face, assessing me, it seemed.

I felt self-conscious, being stared at like that, and it made me clumsy. The fork clattered from my hand onto the plate, and I hurriedly retrieved it. "Oops! Silly me," I chided myself.

Duncan waved his fork at me. "Are you an armchair detective or something, Rose? How come you want the specifics?"

I leaped to my own defense, frowning. "I told you. I'm just curious. It's human nature, after all. Geez!" My eyes darted away.

"Okay. I'm sorry. I just got this sudden impression that you were . . . I don't know, that you were pondering a solution. Doing a Nancy Drew."

That idea made me laugh. Tapping my fingers against my chin, I said, "Hmm. Rose Claypool, Amateur Sleuth. I think I like that."

I was only teasing, and Duncan smiled for just an instant.

"Well, forget it," he said. "Whoever killed Sam was desperate. They wouldn't think twice about killing again, and anyone poking her nose in too far could be in serious danger. That's what police are paid for—to put themselves in danger. Let them do their job, okay?" he admonished.

"Duncan, you are entirely too serious for such a young guy. Lighten up!" I leaned across the table and gave him a thwap on the shoulder. "Now, tell me the rest."

He grinned, shaking his head in dismissal. I figured all that gloom-and-doom lecturing was the result of growing up with a father who was a cop. In its own way, his childhood must have been as rough as mine.

"Okay, okay. But there's not much to tell." He sipped his coffee. "From what I hear, Sam had more enemies than friends, although sometimes it's difficult to tell the difference. As board president, he wielded a lot of power. He was a retired executive, you know. That fidgety kind who have spent so many years being somebody's boss, they've forgotten how to be anything else. I never had any trouble from him personally." He paused for thought, his eyes drifting off over my shoulder. "Not much, at any rate. I know it's a cliché to say there's plenty of people who would have been glad to see him dead, but in this case that's a pretty accurate assessment." He snapped his gaze back. "A man walking a dog through the woods found him. The woods aren't fenced, and they're open to the public, so it's easy for people to come and go."

"Too easy," I commented, and he nodded.

"Yes. Security has never been a strong point here. Even now. Anyway, there had been a board meeting that night, the night of the murder, and Sam had just suggested cutting the weekend program to save a few bucks."

"Was it a popular idea?" I asked without looking up. My dessert had disappeared in record time, and I was using the back of my fork to pick up the last shreds of pistachio nuts.

"Naturally not. Students wouldn't like it, and neither did the staff. Some of us supplement our paychecks that way. It's like moonlighting and, these days, more and more of us have come to rely on that extra salary."

Thanks to that generous alumna I could make it. I wouldn't need a second job.

"After the murder everyone in sight was questioned by the police, but no arrest has been made. Of course, the entire college was buzzing with gossip and speculation for days." He grinned, then gave his head a shake. "Some of the students even claimed they heard odd sounds coming from the cemetery. Old Man Felber, haunting the place!"

"Wait a minute. What cemetery?" I was lost.

"There's an old Indian cemetery bordering the college grounds. Bordering the woods, to be precise." He dropped his voice low and reverberated his words when he added, "Just at the spot where the body was found."

A shiver ran down my spine at the spooky thought. My overactive imagination easily conjured up the scene. The woods in darkness. Damp earth underfoot. Shadows of tombstones silhouetted by moonlight. The dog dashing off into the underbrush. Barking, barking. Stepping forward, under the trees, to see what was wrong. . . .

"Rose!"

I jumped, startled out of my macabre daydream.

"You were a million miles away," Duncan told me.

"Sorry," I said, feeling silly. "I was just thinking about what you said. It must have been an awful time for the college, huh?"

Duncan shrugged. "I don't know. It was stressful, that's true. But it's just as stressful now, only in different ways."

I drank the last of my coffee, refusing the refill the waiter offered. "I'd better get home," I told Duncan. "It will take me all evening to get the paint off my hands and out of my hair!"

He leaned over and gently plucked at a strand, examining it carefully in the dim light. "Ah, yes. I see definite evidence of your hard work," he teased.

We paid the bill. I waved away Duncan's offer to buy my dinner. If he did, the event would seem like a date. If he didn't, we'd merely be colleagues sharing a meal. A minor difference? Not to me.

As we walked slowly back to the car, I had another question to ask. "Duncan, after the murder was the weekend program still canceled?"

He came to a stop on the sidewalk, and I joined him, peering into the window of the furniture store. "No, no. It wasn't. It'll be business as usual. Just like every other year. Why?" He frowned, his expression calculating.

I lifted my shoulders. "No reason. I just wondered if some financially strapped professor did in the board president to make sure those three months of classes weren't canceled. You know, desperate for cash. Couldn't afford to lose that money. Gambling debts? A drug habit? Know anyone like that?"

He took two steps in my direction, crossing the space between us. His hands bit into my shoulders with a fierceness that took me by surprise. I opened my mouth to protest and tried to pull away, but he held fast. He looked me smack in the eye, and I realized for the first time that we were exactly the same height.

"Rose, this isn't a joking matter. Look at me! Listen to me! Don't go around asking questions. Maybe the murderer is one of us. I don't know. I wish I did. But if it is and you go blundering around, being nosy—" He broke off, easing his grip but not the harshness of his message. "I wouldn't want you to be the next body in the woods."

I shook my head wordlessly, startled by his reaction and by the truth of what he said. When he released me,

I took a step backward, watching as he unlocked the car door and held it open for me. Moving past him, onto the cracked seat, I wondered at Duncan's vehement response. He was so determined I butt out. So afraid I might accidentally find out something I shouldn't know. But what? Was he protecting someone? Hiding something? It certainly seemed that way.

He made inconsequential chitchat on the way back to the college, and I think I responded accordingly. My imagination had moved into high gear once more, though, and my thoughts—well, they don't bear repeating.

Chapter Five

I don't mind admitting that, for the next several days, I avoided Duncan. I don't take kindly to being told what to do. Or not do.

My curiosity about the murder had been the garden variety, but, thanks to Duncan, it had grown to monstrous proportions. It seems so ironic now. If he hadn't been so adamant, I wouldn't have been so interested. I probably would have overlooked and dismissed incidents that now caught my eye instead.

As I set to work putting the archives in order, I kept a watch out for any news clippings that mentioned Samuel Felber and read them with special interest. I found a few tearsheets from the local paper written at the time of the murder, and those, too, were eagerly devoured. They didn't tell me anything I hadn't already heard, however, which was a great disappointment.

I had finished painting the room by the end of the week and had primed the space where the mural would go. A few warm, sunny days allowed me to fling wide the windows, chasing the combination of dust and fresh paint smells from the room. Each day, I worked until the light grew dim, sorting and clipping and trying to identify items from the files. I started with the heaps of unlabeled material I'd found strewn on cabinet tops and shoved into file folders in the desk. From there, I thought, I'd move to the cabinets themselves, and, by the time I was finished, order would reign in my kingdom. My work went undisturbed for the most part, although several times when I had answered the telephone, there was no one at the end of the line. I once had a phone number only one digit off from the local pizza parlor's. I'd had plenty of these kinds of calls then, so they didn't especially bother me now.

Lily was a frequent visitor during these busy days, stopping by with a cold can of soda and a bag of potato chips for each of us. I'd take a break, sitting on a rickety wooden folding chair I found in the archives' tiny closet while she parked herself in the newer desk chair.

From her, I learned Dr. Brossman was out of town, attending a conference on higher education. When he returned next week, she told me, the O'Briens' gift would be officially presented to the school. There would be a champagne reception for the staff, our benefactors, and all the local media people.

"What to wear, what to wear," she mused, a chip dangling limply from her hand. "It should be a great opportunity for people watching," she told me, looking at me cautiously.

"Did you have anyone special in mind?"

She looked into her chip bag, rattling it for distraction. "No," she said. "I thought you might, though." Her eyes glanced up at me from under her brows, and I pressed my lips together tight.

Lily knew about my dinner with Duncan. I'd told her just about everything, leaving out only his dire warning. Apparently she thought she heard more in the story.

I sighed, crumpling my empty bag and lobbing it overhand into the trash bin. "Lily, whatever you're thinking, stop." I held her eyes with mine, hoping to force my point home. "I'm not in the market for romance right now. And even if I were, he wouldn't be my choice. Got it?"

Lily nodded. "Sure, Rose, sure. But you know what Shakespeare said." Hand over her heart, eyes lifted skyward, she intoned, "Methinks she doth protest too much."

"Yes, well, not in this case." My words were brusque, but that didn't faze Lily. *A steamroller wouldn't faze her, either,* I thought with amusement.

"I don't know, Rose. I've got a funny feeling," she said, her low voice pitched higher and all sing-songy.

"It's heartburn from all the junk you eat," I joked.

Thankfully, that ended the discussion of that topic, and as she chattered on, I tamped down thoughts of Duncan. It was her fault he'd even come to mind, I told myself. Her fault entirely.

Just a few days later I stopped in the mailroom to check my box. It was early morning, and traffic in the little room was heavy. I recognized Duncan's writing at once, even though I'd never seen it before. My name was printed on an envelope in firm, bold strokes, and I opened it right there.

He was requesting a meeting to discuss his needs for the centennial displays. *Perhaps lunch?* he wrote.

The note was short and to the point, and I hurriedly replied. Crossing out my name, I wrote his underneath and suggested a time and day, then put the envelope into his drawer.

I carried the rest of my mail into the commons and got a cup of coffee before settling in to read it. The student newspaper. Meeting notices. Something from the personnel office about retirement pensions. Only two items were addressed to me personally, and I separated them from the others.

On one, my name was written in a delicate, gossamer hand. A little bunch of flowers had been sketched in one corner, and I wasn't surprised to find it was from Emily Welbourne. The art teacher had written to remind me of the Wednesday-evening sketching class. *Missed you last week!* she concluded, underlining the sentence, and my cheeks burned in embarrassment.

I'd been too tired after my day's work to drag myself to the night class and had spent the time soaking in a tub of hot bubbles. *This week,* I vowed, *I'll be there with bells on!* I even took my monthly planner from my briefcase and added the notation. Now I'd be sure to remember.

The second item was simply a piece of paper folded in half. My name was typed on the front, and the message inside was typewritten as well. One sentence, unsigned.

LEAVE WELL ENOUGH ALONE.

Duncan. Cheap scare tactics, like some old movie.

I folded the note carefully over and tucked it into my planner. Even though my blood was racing through my veins, I felt calm. I wasn't frightened. I wasn't even angry. Well, maybe just a little.

Overkill, I thought, then cringed at my word choice. Still, I wouldn't be frightened away by a little piece of paper. *Sticks and stones,* I thought, reaching for the student newspaper.

Soon I found myself happily engrossed in club minutes, teacher profiles, and pages of surprisingly good poetry. One in particular stuck in my mind. It was a mournful lament, addressing the past, bringing to mind the plight of the Native American artifacts. The author, a student named Karen Waite, had captured the gist of my discussion with Duncan, and I wondered who she was. Lily might know, I decided, thinking I'd mention it the next time I saw her. Draining the last of my coffee, I stashed my mail in my briefcase and headed off to the archives and the endless sorting that awaited me there.

The little typewritten note burned a hole in my thoughts.

"Thanks for meeting me, Rose," Duncan said, holding a chair out for me.

I sat down, briefcase at my side, and said, "No problem. I'm glad we could both make it today."

Several days had passed since I'd received his invitation in the mail, and the time we'd designated for our caucus had arrived. We'd chosen to meet in the commons rather than the archives or an office. That had been my idea, and now, surrounded by the chatter of other people, I didn't regret it. I'd deliberately chosen a table by the window, so I could bask in the sun's warmth, even if it meant I had to squint a little.

Duncan had great plans for the centennial and explained each one, passing me an outline of the schedule of activities.

"This hasn't been approved by the college yet," he told me, leaning over to drag his finger down the page, "but I'm hoping they'll go along."

"I can't see why they wouldn't," I told him. The list was filled with positive publicity-inducing things. Nothing looked the least bit objectionable.

"Yeah, but you can never tell. They wanted to let the anniversary pass with no notice at all."

I shook my head, surprised. "But it's such a good chance to get Lunham's name out in front of the public! Generate some interest and more donations."

Duncan smiled, one corner of his mouth sliding up. The sun was coming over his shoulder, making his hair gleam in the light. In spite of the heavy glasses he wore and despite my smoldering anger at his high-handed attitude, I had to admit, he was a good-looking man.

The thought caught me off guard, and I returned my eyes to the papers in front of me, clearing my throat.

"Boy, it'll be worth the price of admission to see Brossman's face if we get another ancient Bible!" Duncan joked.

"He didn't seem too excited," I admitted.

"What an understatement!" Duncan uncorked a highlighting pen and attacked a closely printed document with it. The pungent smell of the ink drifted across the table, reminding me to redo my nail polish. "I talked to Brossman, you know," Duncan went on. "Said I bet he'd rather have the money than the Bible, and he didn't deny it." He glanced up quickly, waved the pen for emphasis, then returned it to the page. "He told me the ribbon marker is said to be worth even more than the Bible—and the Bible is valued at ten grand!"

I whistled, long and low. I'd only been at the school about a week, but it was easy to see where ten or twenty thousand dollars could go.

"What else did he say?"

"He said with that kind of money, we could get the roof fixed and the heating overhauled." He set his elbows on the table and looked a little forlorn. "I'll tell you, Rose, I don't relish the coming of winter. It's freezing in here. Your feet just never get warm."

I nodded in sympathy although it was hard to picture winter when the trees outside the window were a blaze of autumn colors and the grass still rippled under a warm southwest breeze.

Duncan saw me gazing dreamily out the window and glanced over his shoulder to see what the attraction was. "Beautiful day," he told me.

I turned his own phrase back on him. "What an understatement!"

He thought a moment. "Um, listen. We could discuss this just as easily moving. Would you like to walk?" He jerked his head, indicating the great outdoors.

I was on my feet in a twinkling. "You don't have to ask me twice!" Moving quickly, I started to collect my piles of papers into one bigger pile.

"Oh, leave it. No one will take it. C'mon." Duncan was already standing up, hands shoved into the pockets of his casual fleece sweatshirt.

"What? Leave our stuff?" Such a trusting gesture was foreign to me and seemed risky, even in the closed environment of the school. I opened and shut my mouth, like a fish, looking from my precious stuff to Duncan to the siren song of nature just beyond the window.

"Rose, come on. Trust me."

Trust you? I thought. *Trust you!*

"Okay," I said.

Outside, with the breeze dancing in my hair and filling my lungs with cool, clean air, I felt instantly happy and energetic. We started off at a brisk pace, with Duncan naturally leading the way.

He kept up a steady stream of conversation regarding his plans, picking up where he'd left off in the commons. I tried valiantly to listen, but it was difficult. Just above our heads, the sky was so blue, filled with those puffy white clouds you can see shapes in when you're a child. As we drew nearer the woods, the bird song was deafening. The trees were filled with the bustle of activity, and I stopped on the little dirt path to watch and listen.

It only took Duncan a few moments to realize he'd lost his audience, and he lapsed into silence beside me. Shoulder to shoulder, we stood in the wooded area, surrounded by voices not our own. If I'd been tense at all over this meeting, wondering when to bring up the silly typewritten note, that tension slipped away from me now. I could feel it drop from my shoulders as certainly as if it were an article of clothing to remove.

My breath came out in a sigh of extreme pleasure, and I tipped my head back so the sun fell full on my face. Closing my eyes, I saw patterns of orange and red against my eyelids, the colors dappled as the wind shifted the tree branches above.

I think I would have forgotten I wasn't alone just then if I hadn't felt Duncan's hand brush mine. Tentatively at first, his fingers reached out, bumping my hand in a way that could have been accidental. I didn't pull away, didn't flinch when he became a bit bolder and took my hand firmly in his. My skin grew warmer where he touched me, and my hand felt lost, surrounded by his flesh. That rosy, toasty feeling came over me again, every bit as lovely as the heat of the sun.

I ruined it then. Couldn't help myself. It just seemed like the right time. Squeezing his fingers, I said companionably, "You don't have to send me threatening notes, you know."

"Huh?" He squeezed back, and I could feel his eyes on me.

I blinked a few times, focusing slowly back on my surroundings. "That note. 'Leave well enough alone,' " I quoted.

Duncan took a step back, away from me, still holding my hand. He dipped his head and regarded me with blatant confusion. "Rose, what are you talking about?"

This time when I sighed, there was a hint of exasperation in the gesture. "The same day I got your note about this meeting, I got another note too," I told him, explaining my remark. As I gave him the details, he shook his head, frowning.

"No, Rose. That wasn't from me. I'd never do that." He gave a laugh, hollow and self-deprecating. "I'm no coward, Rose. You should realize that by now. If something is on my mind, I just blurt it out. I'm not the kind for mind games."

"No," I agreed. "I guess you aren't."

It had been so easy to blame Duncan. It seemed so logical at the time. Now, seeing his wide-eyed look of bafflement, hearing it reflected in his denial, I reassessed my evidence. And came up empty. I'd jumped to a conclusion.

"Oh, well, sorry." I shrugged, as if the issue were of little importance.

He opened his mouth, perhaps to caution me again. The look in my eyes must have stopped him, though. "Hmm," he said, reaching up to give his glasses a push. "I don't like the sound of that, Rose."

"Neither do I," I confessed. "But let's not make too much of it. At least, not until I know more."

"Know more? More what?"

We'd begun walking again, following the narrow trail that wound through the woods. Duncan had told me the woods went back quite a way from the college, and it certainly seemed so now.

Lifting my shoulders, I hedged, saying in all honesty, "I don't know that yet, do I? When I do, you'll be the first person I tell." I slipped my hand from his to push away a tree branch, then put it in my pocket. Too much of that toasty feeling would make me very warm, after all.

The trees began to thin out, and I was surprised to see a service road cutting a swath through the woods. To our right, the road disappeared over the top of a hill. To the left, it curved out of sight, presumably to the highway beyond.

We stepped out onto the gravel road and paused. We'd come a long way. This seemed like a good place to turn back.

I said, "I hate to go back. It's so lovely here." My arms spread wide, gathering in the beautiful woods and each one of its residents.

Duncan caught my mood, understanding instantly how I felt. I could see his comprehension in his eyes, framed by the heavy glasses. As if he saw me looking at those ugly black frames, his hand came up, pushing at the nosepiece.

"You should get those things fixed," I told him. "In fact, if you don't mind my saying, you should get a new pair. Something a bit more stylish. And with thinner lenses." Impulsively I reached up, plucking the offending article from his face. Lofting their cumbersome weight in one hand, I went on, "You're a good-looking guy, Duncan, but you hide it with these." As I spoke, I turned to look at him, realizing the true extent of my comment.

The frames had made a heavy red dent across the top of Duncan's incredibly straight nose. Without the black line breaking up his features, I could see cheekbones, gently puffed cheeks, and creases at the corners of his eyes. And those eyes!

I stepped forward to get a better look, marveling at the length of his lashes. *Why,* I thought, *don't I have lashes like that?*

"Oh, Duncan." I shook my head, twirling the frames in one hand. "You've got to get some contact lenses!"

He blushed, cheeks growing rosy, and looked down at our shoes. "Thanks, Rose. That'll do." Stretching out a hand, he waggled his fingers. "Give me the glasses."

"Must I?" I teased, holding them behind my back.

"Yes, you must. I don't really need them, you know. It's just plain glass." He made a swipe at the glasses, but I danced out of reach, feeling mischievous. "At my last job there was a bit of trouble. One of my students. Just a harmless crush, but so embarrassing. So awkward." Another swipe, another miss. We were in the middle of the service road now. "I figured, if I wore these. . . ." He trailed off, coloring again.

"If you wore these, the students wouldn't realize how handsome you are," I finished for him.

"Well, yeah." He was reluctant to agree. "Not that I'm conceited or anything."

I shook my head. "Just telling the truth."

He took a step closer, slowly putting both arms around me to the small of my back. His glasses dangled from my hands there, and he covered my hands with his. We were very close now, our bodies barely inches apart. The teasing humor had gone out of the moment, and I stood stock still, afraid to move.

It seemed the songs of the birds grew louder as Duncan drew near, as if they were excited as well. I held my breath, looking into his eyes. Everything in me was shouting for joy during this moment of delightful anticipation. Still, a dissenting voice intruded, bringing my own words back to me.

"I'm not interested in romance," I'd told Lily. *"And if I were, Duncan wouldn't be my choice."*

Oh, shut up, I thought just as Duncan tipped his head. I waited until his mouth was hovering above mine, then allowed my eyes to close.

His kiss was thorough, not hesitant or questioning. The pressure of his lips started a tingle deep inside of me. He tightened his hold on me, moving his hands to my waist.

Even when you're not looking for love, there are times when it just feels so right. This moment was one of those. Maybe tomorrow I'd regret it. Maybe five minutes from now it would seem like a mistake. But, oh, oh, there was a thumping from my heart and a roaring in my ears!

That roar got louder, and I realized in a heartbeat it wasn't caused by blood rushing through my veins. When I opened my eyes, I froze in a panic. Coming over the top of the hill at a speed unsafe on any highway was a monstrous black car. It seemed to be all grill and headlights as it raced toward us. We were standing directly in its path. Duncan couldn't see the danger. His back was toward the vehicle.

Acting on impulse and adrenaline, I sprung into motion. Grasping Duncan's shoulders, I spun him to face the edge of the road, then jumped forcefully against him from behind. He cried out in surprise as we fell haphazardly into the brush lining the service drive. I heard the powerful roar of the engine as the car streaked past us, having never even tried to slow down. I looked over my shoulder and had a quick impression of a chrome bumper with a big red sticker on the right-hand side and a bright yellow license plate. There was a splash of yellow at the passenger window as well. Two people, then, driving too fast, coming over that blind hill, never expecting people to be there, unable to stop. It rocketed by, and I could feel the displaced air swish near my feet in a gust, sending the fall leaves swirling in its wake.

Duncan hit the ground first, with me half clinging to him. All the air rushed out of me when I landed, coming out on a sound like, "Oof!"

There was a slight decline in this part of the woods, and we rolled over a few times before stopping. The sky whirled by my eyes, then trees, then the sleeve of Duncan's coat as I tumbled. When we came to rest, it took us a moment to catch our breath, and in that time I could make out the fading sounds of the automobile as it reached the highway beyond the trees.

"What the—" Duncan began, struggling into an upright position. He had bits of leaves tangled in his hair and a smear of mud down one cheek. I figured I probably looked the same.

Sitting up, I felt my fear replaced by anger and exploded, "Did you see that idiot? He nearly killed us! What would he be doing on a service drive in the first place, and why in blazes was he doing eighty?" The words tumbled over each other in their rush to get out, and Duncan moved quickly to my side.

"Take it easy, take it easy," he purred, putting his arm around my shoulders. Resting one dirt-streaked palm against my cheek, he held my head gently to his chest, cooing and smoothing my hair while I took deep breaths and waited for my pulse to slow. "You know, I think you saved my life just now, Rose," he told me. His voice was low and steady, but his hands were definitely shaking, and I could barely hear him over the hammering of his heart. "I think that means I'll always be indebted to you."

I gave a tremulous smile. He was trying to comfort me, lightening the mood and making me see the danger was past. I was safe. He was safe. An involuntary shudder shook me and I sighed with a quiver.

Pushing against Duncan, I sat up beside him and ran both hands through my jumbled hair. "I'm okay, Duncan," I assured him. "Shaken but unhurt."

Duncan nodded. "Me too. Did you see who was driving? What make was the car?"

"Are you kidding? All I saw was this huge grill coming over that hill too fast to stop without creaming us." I shook my head. "I'd give my eyeteeth to know what nut was behind that wheel so I could bring him in for reckless driving! We could have been killed!"

Duncan stood up and brushed at his clothing, then extended a hand to me. He pulled me to my feet, and I, too, did my best to remove the leaves and bits of grass clinging to me. "Well, it's not like it was deliberate, Rose," Duncan said, trying to be rational. "That's a bad spot, the hill blocks the view. We were in the wrong place at the wrong time, that's all."

"That may be, but it doesn't excuse such chaotic driving," I muttered.

"Too bad we're so far from the parking lot," Duncan said. "We could have followed him otherwise. Maybe gotten the plate number."

We'd advanced to the edge of the service drive now and carefully looked both ways before crossing.

"Wait a minute. In your car?" I wrinkled my nose. "You must be joking. By the time you got it started, he'd be in the next county." I laughed out loud, picturing the scene. Duncan's old beater wheezing out of the college parking lot and onto the highway, leaving a trail of blue smoke in the air.

"That car is just fine, Rose. It may need a tune-up, but it always passes the emission test."

"You're kidding," I scoffed, following him on the narrow path through the woods. We were retracing our steps now, not lingering to enjoy the scenery but moving rapidly, anxious to get back.

"No, I'm not. You shouldn't be so hung up on appearances, Rose. Don't judge people on the basis of material goods. Those things don't last."

"Thank you, Sigmund Freud," I drawled, and he shot me a glance over one shoulder.

"Tell me about the car. Would you recognize it if you saw it again?"

I shook my head. "I don't know. I don't think so. There was someone wearing yellow in the passenger seat, I know that. It had a yellow license plate." I closed my eyes and stopped on the path, trying to bring that fleeting image to mind. "You know, like the kind on government vehicles. And . . . and there was some kind of sticker on the bumper. Square. Red. I've seen it before. Where? Where?"

It was frustrating. The vision dangled on the edge of my brain, tauntingly close but elusive. I sighed, conceding defeat, and in that rush of air, I remembered.

"Duncan! It was the same as that sticker on your car! Next to that old peace sign—you know the one!" I grabbed his arm and gave it a brisk shake.

"That one? That's a permit for the parking garage at the county building."

"See! A government office building! A government license!" I crowed, as if I'd proven something.

Duncan was quick to raise a doubt. "That office building is mostly given over to government, true. But the top two floors aren't. They're just offices. Realtors, dentists, charity groups."

"Oh." We went a way in silence, each of us tumbling the matter over, I'm sure. Finally I said, "How do you know?"

Duncan shrugged, and I noticed a torn seam at the shoulder of his jacket. "That's where the Native American group meets. The one that held the picket. Since I always attend the meetings, I have a parking sticker. Everyone in the group does."

"Oh," I said again, thoroughly deflated.

We burst through the last of the woods and crossed the grass toward the college. My body was starting to ache now, and I began to favor one knee.

"I wouldn't see too much mystery in this if I were you," Duncan told me. "It was probably just somebody who got lost and was in a hurry."

He was so calm about our brush with disaster. My adrenaline still pumped, and I wondered why fate had seen fit to interrupt our romantic interlude with a potentially fatal accident. A memorable moment, to be sure.

"Well, whoever it was, they spoiled our walk," I pouted.

Chapter Six

I sat at the little desk in the archives, lost in another, older world. This was the reason I'd become an archivist. This was why my favorite reading material was historical biography. To me, there is no sensation finer than catching a glimpse of how life was lived hundreds of years ago. Or a hundred years ago, in this case, since the material I studied was the charter for Lunham College.

Carefully I sifted through the documents, wearing thin cotton gloves to prevent the oils on my skin from getting on the paper. These pages were already pretty far gone, but I had to do what I could. I looked in horror at a torn corner that had been haphazardly mended with cello tape. The tape, of course, had turned yellow and brittle. Pieces of it fell into my lap when I lifted the paper.

The charter made fascinating reading and gave me an interesting insight on the past. From what I read, I learned that the land for Lunham College had been owned by one of the Native American tribes in the area. A treaty between them and Joseph Lunham had resulted in Lunham's acquisition of the land. He'd paid the tribe the princely sum of sixty dollars per person. It must have seemed like a fortune then.

Fingering the charter, I wondered if a copy of that treaty was around. Tucked in one of the numerous, unlabeled manila folders, perhaps? Shoved in a cabinet, wrinkled and musty?

Duncan would love a copy of this for his display, I thought, reluctantly setting it aside and moving on. I'd make sure he got one soon, along with copies of the architect's drawings for the college chapel. Another lost treasure, the delicately rendered sketches were a work of art on their own. I'd admired them at great length, picking out the different architectural styles I could see. Gothic windows, Norman columns, and a bit of Victorian bric-a-brac, the various elements combined not into the expected mishmash, but into a charming and regal place of worship.

The notes attached to the drawings informed me the brick for the structure had been trucked from a quarry clear across the state. Stained-glass windows had been handcrafted by a European artisan known for his intricate and breathtaking designs. One hundred years ago it would have been a delight, tucked among the trees. Now, having aged to a golden patina, the creamy brick of the chapel would glow in the setting sun, looking like a bit of rural England.

Joseph Lunham had had money and plenty of it, I figured, if he could purchase all that land and commission individual windows.

I'd seen the steeple of the chapel poking up through the woods near the college but hadn't gotten any closer yet. *Some lunch hour,* I thought, *I'll walk over and take a peek.* Not today, though.

Today I'd spend my free period walking the half mile to my apartment to change into suitable attire for the afternoon's gala event. The O'Briens would be here, along with all the local media, to officially present the ancient Bible to the college. We were all expected to be present and accounted for, bedecked in our Sunday best.

I was looking forward to it, actually. A champagne reception, hors d'oeuvres, the whole ball of wax. To my way of thinking, there aren't enough opportunities in this world for dressing up. I planned on wearing my best red dress. A knit with a fitted bodice and sweetheart neckline, it had a full sweeping skirt that brushed at my ankles. I wore it with a wide gold belt and gold jewelry and carried my black Chanel quilted bag.

In that outfit I felt sophisticated and elegant, although I had to work hard to act that way. This afternoon I planned to keep my mouth shut and my eyes open. If I were observant, maybe I could spot someone who felt a need to warn me to "leave well enough alone." The dynamic interaction between people was always fascinating, and a watchful eye could glean plenty of nonverbal information.

With this goal in mind, I joined the throng entering the college auditorium several hours later, standing up very straight to do justice to that red dress. Once everyone had settled into the theaterlike seats the lights dimmed and conversations dwindled into silence.

Dr. Brossman took center stage, standing behind a wooden lectern with the college logo on the front. After making a few opening remarks and grinning rather obviously at the gathered handful of photographers, he introduced our guests of honor.

The O'Briens had been seated on heavy ornamental chairs at stage left. Now they came forward as we applauded politely. Dr. Brossman maneuvered his bulk from behind the lectern, and Mr. O'Brien handed over the antique Bible. Dr. Brossman took it rather cautiously, like a bachelor holding a newborn. He oohed and aahed a bit, being a politician, after all.

I should have been listening to Mr. O'Brien's words as he made the presentation, but instead I spent a good five minutes admiring the couple's upper-class looks and demeanor. Well-dressed, well-groomed, they oozed a perfect vision of the American Dream in old age. Mrs. O'Brien's silver hair gleamed as if polished. The buttons of her natty two-piece suit shone with what may have been real gold. Mr. O'Brien wore a five-hundred-dollar pinstripe job, molded to shoulders still wide, but concealing that standard businessman's paunch.

As I daydreamed over what life must be like as one of the rich folks, the little ceremony concluded and everyone was clapping again. We filed back out, jammed in the main aisle like the freeway during rush hour, and headed for a conference room that had been cleared for the event. Within minutes we were all milling around, holding little plastic cups of champagne. Students and staff clustered in small groups, and the atmosphere was light.

I scanned the crowd and spotted Lily in conversation with a woman I'd seen briefly around the school. Drink in hand, I joined them. Lily introduced the woman as Professor Georgia Spencer of the philosophy department.

"You've got the office across the hall from me!" I told her, remembering the name from the plate on the door.

Georgia nodded and smiled, but her eyes shifted away instantly. She was a few inches shorter than I and about ten pounds heavier. Her curly red hair fell in a cascade to the middle of her back. Her suit, a hot pink that should have clashed with her hair but didn't, was cut to emphasize a decidedly hourglass figure.

I glanced at Lily, who merely shrugged, and we both looked off to see what Georgia found so fascinating. About twenty feet away, just visible through the crowd, Duncan was chatting with Emily Welbourne. The art teacher shook a gnarly finger at him, and he chuckled, putting his arm around her.

Seeing Duncan, and Georgia's unrestrained observation of him, connected the two in my mind. Then I recalled my first day at the college and my first encounter with Duncan. He'd come flying out from across the hall after getting into a shouting match. His opponent must have been Georgia Spencer. This interesting twist dredged up several questions at once, and I didn't realize my eyes had glazed over until Lily gave me a firm nudge.

Georgia was making typical murmurs of interest in my job, and I made the typical responses. Quite a challenge. Enjoying it sincerely. Making steady progress. We went on in this vein for several minutes, until we'd exhausted all the social platitudes.

"Well"—Georgia swept a glance around once more—"I think I've put in enough of an appearance. See you around." To me, "It was a pleasure to meet you."

Lily and I waved her off, watching her melt into the crowd.

"Friend of yours?" I asked.

"Who? Georgia?" Lily seemed surprised by the suggestion. Her eyebrows shot up, and she shook her head, almost laughing but not with amusement. "Oh, no, Rose. Georgia is a friend to no one. She occasionally descends to our level, but never for long and never for real."

"I did rather get that impression," I told her.

"Yes. Georgia's personal philosophy is 'Don't tread on me.' " Lily laughed, low and husky.

I smiled, wondering if Georgia and Duncan were or ever had been an item. I pride myself on speaking my mind. If something bothers me, I usually don't hesitate to say so. If I'm curious about something, I ask. But I wouldn't ask Lily. I'd go right to the horse's mouth.

Glancing across the room, I saw Emily, but Duncan had moved on, working the room quite efficiently.

"You know, I'm going to take off too," I told Lily, emptying my glass in one last swallow. "I need to stop in the library for a research book."

"Oh?" Lily pursed her lips.

"Personal research. Idle curiosity," I confessed. "One of the clippings I ran across recently said the college and its founder were mentioned in a book. *At the Meeting of the Rivers*. Ever hear of it?"

She shook her head.

"I just thought I'd see if we have it and what it says. Just for fun."

"Some fun," Lily drawled. "Reading ancient history." She mocked a yawn, hand over her mouth, eyes blinking slowly.

It was my turn to shake my head. "I'll see you later."

With plenty of smiles and excuse me's, I was able to weave my way to the door. After the noisy chatter of the crowded room, the silence of the vacant, carpeted hallway was very pleasant. As I walked toward the stairwell, only the muffled sound of my shoes reached my ears, and I gave a sigh. I hadn't realized how anxious I was to escape that crowd until now, when it was behind me.

I pushed open the door to the stairs and headed down, my steps clattering and echoing in the enclosed space. In the time I'd been here, I'd worked hard to learn my way around and knew this particular flight of steps would put me just down the hall from the library.

Only a student working at the circulation desk was in evidence as I entered. Everyone else was still at the reception, apparently. The card catalog directed me to the book I wanted, and it waited there on the shelf. Its original cover had long since vanished, and the book had been rebound in an unattractive blue imitation leather. I leafed through it briefly, then decided to check it out and take it with me.

The girl at the desk was issuing me a library card when Harriet marched through the double doors.

"Well, well, Ms. Claypool!" the librarian exclaimed, coming to stand next to me. She took in the situation at a glance, tipping her head to read the title on the spine of my book. "Oh, fascinating reading," she assured me, tapping the cover. "You'll enjoy it."

"Thanks," I said, smiling at her and looking away rapidly. She had a disturbing way of holding your eye, boring into you and making you squirm. Harriet, I decided, was not a pleasant person.

"How goes the war?" she asked me now, dragging on our encounter. "Making progress in the . . . what did you call it? Disaster area?" Her tone was sharp, critical.

"I don't think I ever said that," I responded, then added, "but it would be a pretty accurate description of what I found."

Her eyes narrowed a bit, then flared wide. "I'm sure you'll soon set it to rights. And what's this I hear about a mural? Do you really think that's necessary?"

"Necessary, no. But it will be a lovely addition. I'm so grateful to Ms. Welbourne for suggesting it," I gushed, sincerity lending strength to my words. "It will add just the right note of historical significance to the room, give people a real sense of the past."

Harriet lifted her bony shoulders. "It would seem to me Ms. Welbourne has enough work of her own to do these days."

I couldn't help myself, although I didn't even try. I said, "Yes, but we all wear many hats here at Lunham, you know. We all help each other out. One big, happy family." I smiled, thanked the student as she handed me my library card, and nodded a farewell to Harriet. "Feel free to stop in anytime," I told her as I stepped toward the door.

She nodded but said nothing. If looks could kill, I'd have expired right there, I think.

Clutching my precious volume, I walked slowly down the hall, wondering why she was so critical and nosy. Was she like that with everyone or just with me? And, if it was just me, what had I done—or not done—to earn her wrath?

There was more than one mystery at Lunham College, it would seem.

Chapter Seven

The college was quiet and eerie at night. It was Wednesday, the evening of Emily's sketching class, so I'd returned after working hours. The hallways, dim even during the day, were in near darkness now. An unseen cleaning crew had passed through recently. The scent of pine cleaner hung in the air. A distant, indistinguishable sound led me easily to the art department, and as I drew nearer, it flattened out to the murmur of conversation. Light spilled into the hallway from the classroom, and I paused at the doorjamb to peek inside.

The big room had the expected high ceiling. Four wide, square tables filled each corner of the room, leaving the middle area free. A chair sat there now, waiting for tonight's subject, I supposed. About a dozen people were milling around, examining the day students' works in progress and debating the merits of talent and style.

Emily looked up from the cupboard where she'd been retrieving supplies, and when she saw me, a smile of pleasure and surprise lit her face.

"Rose, dear!" she exclaimed, sweeping her arms in an invitation. "Come in! Come in! I'm glad you could make it!" She crossed the room in my direction, and I headed for her, meeting her halfway. She gave my arms a squeeze and impulsively touched her cheek to mine. A faint scent of lavender reached me, mingling with the heady aromas of oil paint and rubber cement already perfuming the air. "We're just getting ready to start. Why don't you sit here?" she suggested, her hand at the small of my back, propelling me to the far side of the room.

The others—students, a few faculty members, and some elderly folks who must have been friends of Emily's—broke into small groups and took places at each table. Smiles were exchanged, and I made small talk with the two men at my table, discussing our art experience as Emily scurried around with pencils and paper.

Across from me sat a young girl I'd seen frequently in the halls and in the commons. I knew she was a student, but that was all, and it didn't seem as if I'd learn more tonight. When I smiled a greeting in her direction, the edges of her lips turned up, as if she wanted to smile but didn't complete the effort. Her silence matched her rather solemn expression, and she looked away, her pencil moving over the edges of her paper in rapid-fire doodling.

When she tipped her head, a long curtain of glossy black hair obscured her features. She wore it parted down the middle in a manner that drew attention to her close-set eyes and larger than fashionable nose. Her appearance may not have fit conventional standards of beauty, but there was a dignified, almost regal bearing to her posture, her movements, even the way she held her pencil. Unlike so many young people grappling with finding a place in the world, she seemed to have a healthy sense of self-esteem. Her silence wasn't due to shyness, but natural reserve, a very different characteristic.

My attention was drawn away when Emily stood in the center of the room and clapped her hands briskly.

"All right, class, let's get started!" she called out. "Tonight we'll be doing our own little version of Rodin's famous "Thinker," and I *think*"—she stressed the word, drawing a chuckle from her students—"that you'll all recognize tonight's model." Addressing me, she added, "We all take turns being the subject."

"Oh." Here was a twist. When my turn rolled around, I'd be sure to be absent. I could never hold still that long. And the "Thinker"—well. . . .

There was movement near the doorway, and as Emily sang, "Here's Duncan!" in he strode.

Collectively we gave a gasp, followed almost immediately by discreet chuckling.

Shoulders back, head held high, he entered like a warrior. His expression, aiming for cool disdain, was one of barely concealed mirth instead.

And with good reason.

Attired in only a bathing suit of the skimpier variety, he was exposing a lot of pink flesh to our stunned gaze. I took in at a glance those broad shoulders and that muscular, fuzzy chest. He had just a hint of the ripples Schwartzenegger boasted, neatly dividing his stomach. I tightened mine automatically and sat up a little straighter. Narrow hips led to fuller legs and admirably defined calves.

I pursed my lips and gave a wolf whistle in appreciation. As the others laughed outright, Duncan turned his eyes to me and gave a start.

Of course, he had no reason to expect me here, I thought. *Any more than I expected him.* I delivered my best saucy wink, and he colored, cheeks flushing pink in a manner I found both endearing and adorable.

"All right! All right! That will do!" Emily scolded. The smile on her face contrasted with her discipline, but we all settled in obediently.

With great care Duncan was arranged in a pose to mimic the famous sculpture. When Emily was satisfied, she stood back, tipped her head to one side, and circled around him, checking every angle once more. She looked at the clock and announced, "We'll take forty-five minutes for this study, class. You may begin."

At first it was difficult for me. Ages had passed since I'd last attempted a serious work. Also, I couldn't see the model as just a model. For the first ten minutes I saw Duncan and, of course, that affected my work. As I progressed, however, the pencil began to feel more comfortable in my grasp, and I was able to observe with an artist's eye.

Long ago an instructor had told me to draw not what was there but what wasn't there. In the manner of a sculptor seeing a statue in a block of marble and chiseling away all the bits that surrounded it, I struggled on, sketching in the space between Duncan's elbow and stomach, the curve at the back of his bent knee.

Emily wandered the room slowly, pausing beside each of us to watch our drawings emerge. A few times I heard her point out trouble spots or make encouraging remarks. Many times, she merely "Mm-hmm"-ed and patted a shoulder.

By the time she got to my side of the room, I'd made a good start and gotten down an outline I was pleased with. I wasn't so pleased, however, with the detail of his clenched fist. Propped against his chin, it looked little like human flesh on my page and more like a gnarled bit of tree root. Furrowing my brow, I added a few more lines—and made matters worse.

"Here," Emily said in a whisper. She leaned over my paper and applied her own pencil, narrating as she went so she was certain I understood. "So . . . and so." Her pencil flicked lightly against the page, a feather here and there, and immediately what had been hard grew soft. What was unnatural took on life. My tree root became recognizable as five fingers wrapped around and tucked in.

I shook my head in amazement. I'd never be an artist. I simply didn't possess that degree of talent. When Emily gave my shoulder a pat, it was one of consolation.

At the break, Duncan unfurled from his bent position and gave a mighty stretch. As the class stood and chatted, examining one another's work, he slipped out the door, returning a few minutes later more conventionally attired in jeans and a cotton sweater.

"Fancy meeting you here," he said, pulling up a chair next to mine. "May I?" He gestured at my drawing, and I shrugged.

"Don't expect much."

He pursed his lips, nodding his head now and then as his eyes flicked over my interpretation. "It's good, Rose," he told me. "You're just rusty. Maybe you aren't da Vinci, but I hope you won't give up." His eyes locked with mine, and my heart started to thump.

"I won't," I told him, taking the paper from his hand and fiddling with the corner. "I enjoy it too much."

"Maybe the still life will be easier," he suggested.

"Let's hope so." I laughed, watching Emily wheel out an arrangement of wax fruit and wine bottles.

An hour later I sat back, pleased. I may have even smiled a bit as I held my paper at arm's length. *Not bad,* I thought.

"Not bad," Duncan echoed and held up his own.

Different eyes see different scenes, make different interpretations of the same material—a lesson I was to learn time and time again. Although we'd drawn the same items, our sketches were chalk and cheese. That didn't bother me, though, and I stacked my sketches together, still smiling.

After returning our pencils to Emily, Duncan and I took a few moments to wander around the room, examining the work of the college students. Stretched out on a long table against one wall was a felt banner like the kind I'd seen in several stairwells. Obviously Emily's work, it was red, appliqued with patchwork geometric designs, and accented with colored beads and sequins. I ran a hand over it, feeling the sharp edges of the jewels contrasted with the soft material.

"You've got to see this, Rose," Duncan said from a few feet away, his voice laden with excitement. "Every week I check it out, and it just gets better and better."

He took hold of my elbow and brought me to an easel. "Look!"

I did.

The painting was done in oils and filled a canvas nearly three feet square. In the background were woods like those near the college and all over the state. In the foreground, commanding all the viewer's attention, was the stern, handsome face of a young Native American. Deep-black eyes blazed out from under heavy brows, as if he were imparting a message of great importance. The firm set of his jaw brought a sense of anger to the work; since there was no historical setting or context to the painting, he looked both ancient and contemporary.

"It's magnificent!" I exclaimed, leaning closer and reaching out a hand.

"Don't touch it!" Duncan slapped my hand away. "It's still wet."

"I . . . I didn't realize," I said. "The skin looks so lifelike, I wanted to feel it." I smiled, feeling silly.

"She's done an excellent job bringing him to life," Duncan agreed. "But I don't think she'd say thank you if you smudged him."

The possibility truly hadn't occurred to me, I'd been so stunned by the force of the painting. I took a step back.

"She? Did Emily do this?"

"Oh, no. Karen did." Duncan looked over his shoulder and waved a hand. The solemn girl from my table saw the gesture and approached us.

"Karen, I'd like you to meet Rose Claypool. We were just admiring your wonderful warrior here."

We shook hands as Duncan finished the introduction. "Karen is one of my best students and, obviously, one of Emily's best too."

I lavished a few minutes of praise on the artist, and she seemed pleased, but I couldn't be sure. Her eyes kept moving from my face to Duncan's, then past us to the edges of the room, as if the attention made her nervous.

Duncan mentioned that both he and Karen were members of the local Native American activist group. "She's the one who told me about it," he explained.

"Were you at the protest too?" I asked her. "The one at the historical society?"

She nodded, and I thought that was going to be my only answer until she said, "I was there, yes. It was an important event. A first step. A small one. But there will be others." Her lips compressed as she thought for a moment. "You seem interested in our cause, Rose. Perhaps you'd like to join us."

My eyes widened. My activism had always been of the armchair variety. A few letters to my congressperson, a few checks to worthy causes. *Why not?* I thought. *They need me.* I was flattered. I was moved. I said, "Sure. But I don't really know much about the background on this."

"No problem. Come to our next meeting. I'll pick you up," Duncan offered. "Check it out, and if you want to get involved, great. If not,"—he shrugged—"that's your choice too."

An open-ended agreement. My kind of deal. We made it a date.

As Karen turned to leave, she gave a brief smile of farewell and gathered up her coat. It was covered with a geometric pattern of Indian design, and around the collar she swirled a yellow scarf. The scarf caught my eye at once. Yellow. Caution. Danger. That car in the woods. I frowned, but Duncan's voice interrupted my thoughts.

"She likes you," Duncan told me, and I turned to him, surprised. "I've never seen her smile before." He slipped his arm around me, squeezing me at the waist. "Must be magic, hmm?"

I grimaced at his flowery prose and pulled back a little. Duncan readily released me, and I was grateful for the easy way he read my mood.

Nearly all the students had gone by this time. Duncan and I waited around until the last had straggled out and Emily was ready to lock up; then we all walked to the parking lot together. I was glad for the company. The evening had grown cool and windy, with gray clouds obscuring the moonlight. The wind whistled through the crisp leaves that still clung to branches and swirled the fallen ones around our feet. Emily stopped in the middle of the sidewalk and wrapped her sweater more tightly around her shoulders. Then, tipping her head back, she inhaled deeply, her eyes closing in pleasure.

I smiled as I watched her and, inspired, did the same, letting the fresh air fill my lungs and tingle my toes.

"I love the autumn," Emily told us, linking her arm through mine and resuming our walk.

"Me too. With spring a close second," I added.

We reached Emily's car and saw her safely on her way. As her taillights blinked into the distance, Duncan turned to me, putting his arms around me and pulling me close.

"Need a lift?" he asked, and I shook my head, half wishing I could say yes, wondering what would transpire on my doorstep. My toes started tingling again as the thought crossed my mind, and I gave a shiver of delight.

"Then I guess I'll just see you tomorrow." Duncan sounded disappointed, but it didn't stop him from moving closer. As if we'd done it a million times and not just once, our heads turned, removing our noses from the line of action, and then our lips met in a lingering, wonderful kiss.

"Mmm," I said as we parted. "That was lovely."

Duncan smiled that lopsided smile, one corner of his mouth lifting higher than the other. "There's more where that came from," he told me and proved it.

A long time later we separated with reluctance. Duncan waited until I got my car started before going off to his own. I could hear when the engine of his old beater took hold, roaring loudly in the quiet night, and I nearly laughed out loud. That thing was an environmental hazard, not to mention an eyesore. But he claimed it was up to code, and if the government didn't care about the racket and the fumes, who was I to criticize? He spun off in one direction while I took the other, around the back of the school.

Driving at night makes me nervous, even if it's just a short distance, and so I crept along the curvy road behind the main building. It was just coincidence that I happened by at that moment. Just a fluke that I saw a flash of light in a second-floor window. A window I already knew well. The window of the archives.

I stepped on the brake and looked again, blinking. Yes, there was definitely a light on in that room. My mind searched for plausible reasons for someone to be there. Cleaning crew? They'd have long since gone. It was after ten o'clock. My hands clenched and unclenched on the cold steering wheel, and as I watched, the light snapped off.

It's probably nothing, I thought, gnawing on my bottom lip. *Who could it be? No one has any business in there. No one but me.*

It was cold. It was dark. It was late and I was tired. But I was also curious, and curiosity will get the better of me nine times out of ten.

Without even taking a moment to think, I pulled the car into the fire lane directly behind the building, shut off the engine, and pelted up the sidewalk to the door. The key on my ring unlocked it, and I lifted my heels as I scurried down the hall so my shoes wouldn't raise such a clatter.

The hallway outside the archives was silent and dark. I paused, one hand against my chest, to catch my breath. My lungs burned from gulps of cool air I'd taken in during my sprint, and I swallowed a few times.

Looking around at the utter stillness, I felt a moment's qualm. What was I so worried about? All I'd seen— or thought I'd seen—was a light going off. There was nothing sinister in that. Was there?

Trailing my hand along the smooth brick wall, I advanced slowly on the door of the archives. No sound came from within. No light was apparent now. I fumbled in my pocket for my key ring, and the metallic jingle they made seemed to echo in the quiet space.

"Ssh!" I hissed, separating the archives key. It slipped easily into the lock, and the doorknob gave way under my hand.

I pushed the door open but didn't enter at first. Too many television movies and tales of urban crime made me reluctant to frame myself in the doorway as an easy target for some criminal. Snaking a hand around the jamb, I flipped on the light switch, and fluorescent bulbs blinked to life.

Obviously no one was there.

Obviously someone had been.

The acrid smell of cigarette smoke reached my nose as I entered the room, and I gave a sniff of disgust. It hung heavily in the air, recently exhaled, giving me proof of a trespasser's presence. I made certain the door was propped open behind me, then took a quick circle tour of the room. Nothing appeared out of place, although so much sorting and organizing had yet to be done that it was difficult to be sure.

Over near the little desk, the smell of smoke was stronger. I'd worked here just that day, using old rags and page cleaner to remove the soil from some materials. The solvent had a distinctive smell, like that of an orange, and the remnants of the odor still lingered.

I pulled out the desk chair and sat, frowning, wondering what my desk held that someone found fascinating. Who had been here? Why?

The smell of burning seemed thicker now, and I wrinkled my nose, instinctively reaching for the trash can nearby. I'll always wonder whether the cigarette stub I found smoldering there among my discarded rags had been deliberately deposited while lit. It could

have been an accident, I thought later. Simple care-
lessness. My suspicious mind, however, brought up a
more perplexing conclusion.

The cigarette appeared to have been lit and discarded
at once. Very little had burned off, and it was still a good
three inches long. Did smokers light cigarettes and then
throw them away? I didn't know, but it wasn't logical.
Using a paper tissue, I picked up the cigarette, stubbing
it out firmly against the side of the trash can.

If I hadn't come in, I realized as I dropped the offen-
sive object, the smoldering butt may have ignited the
rags. Covered in cleaning fluid, they would certainly
be flammable. I sucked in a breath, looking around the
room at the stacks of brittle paper, ready kindling for a
flame. It wouldn't take long for fire to sweep the room.
By the time the fire alarms and sprinklers went on, con-
siderable damage would be done. Historical documents
would be lost forever.

I took the extra step of removing the rags to another
bin, then checked the room once more for any further
trouble spots. Convinced all was now well, I snapped
off the lights, locked up, and headed home, still puzzling
over this latest incident.

Chapter Eight

When I arrived at work the next morning, Emily was perched on a ladder in the archives, transferring her design for the historical mural from the paper in her hand to the primed walls.

I stopped dead when I saw her—a tiny form, high up on a ladder that looked just as fragile as she did.

"Emily!" I exclaimed by way of greeting. "How did you get in here?" Crossing the room, I tossed my jacket over a chair and pushed up the sleeves of my sweater.

"Oh, good morning, Rose." She turned and looked down at me, smiling brightly. "I had the custodian let me in. About an hour ago. I like to get an early start."

"You certainly do." The sun was out and over the horizon, of course, but it wasn't yet eight o'clock. I moved to the window and pulled the curtains open even farther. Artists need natural light, and it felt good to work in the sun.

"That's lovely, dear," Emily gushed sincerely. "I hope I won't be in your way here this morning, but the centennial celebrations aren't that far off, and I wanted to make a dent in this." She leaned back, her eyes moving from the page to the wall.

I stepped onto the bottom rung of the ladder so I could peer at the paper. The design submitted by Emily for approval by the president was a panoramic view of the college grounds. The buildings were spread in a hollow surrounded by trees. A few people attired in old-fashioned clothing wandered the walkways. A watercolor wash had been applied to give an idea of the color choices—lush greens, soothing blues, and golden, glowing cream. An idealized view of Lunham College, to be sure, but one the administration would be happy to present as factual, both then and now.

"It's gorgeous," I said, reaching over to tap the page. "But what a job! How long will it take?"

"Oh, not that long, really, since we'll have more than one person working on it. Karen and a few other students have volunteered to do the bulk of the job. They'll be contacting you for a schedule of convenient times. I know you wouldn't want anyone in here without your approval or supervision."

I didn't point out that she had come in without my approval. I could hardly fault her enthusiasm, and such a remark would be mean-spirited. Still, a tiny bit of me wished she had waited for me to arrive before starting the project. As a new staff member, I was well aware of my ranking on the totem pole—and her spot as grand dame of the college. If she requested access, there was no reason on earth to deny it.

"Well, I'll just leave you to it." I stepped off the ladder and took my place at the little desk. As my knee collided with the trash bin, I recalled the mysterious incident of the previous evening.

"Emily, do you know which staff members are smokers?" Perhaps the intruder hadn't been part of the faculty, but it seemed like a logical place to start.

"What an unusual question! I don't think I know about everyone, but I do know Georgia Spencer does. Dr. Brossman too. Lily gave it up. There's willpower for you. Duncan never has. Of course, I dabbled in my youth but quickly abandoned the habit. Very expensive and not at all attractive. Why do you ask?" She never stopped to look at me, but kept right on drawing as the words tumbled out.

With no hesitation I told her about my discovery the night before. I wasn't surprised when she pooh-poohed my concern. I was beginning to do the same myself.

"Probably the cleaning staff, Rose. I wouldn't worry about it. You could send a memo of complaint to that department, though, so your concern is documented," she suggested.

"Good idea. I think I will." Scribbling out a note to myself on the pad of paper, I felt better. Taking positive action always improved a situation.

We worked on in silence, Emily humming a melodic tune. The folder I was sorting contained more papers relating to the college chapel, and I integrated them with the others I'd located previously. A good ten minutes or so passed before Emily interrupted her tune.

"Come to think of it," she said, expecting me to follow her train of thought, "the week after that unpleasant murder, several rather odd things happened around the campus."

"Odd?" I set down the papers I held and swiveled my chair around to face her. "Like what? Do you remember?"

"Well, they weren't unexplainable or even very dangerous. More like mischief. Malicious mischief." She leaned forward, closer to the wall, and added another line with a steady hand while I waited for her to continue. "There were a few broken windows. Some anonymous hate mail to Dr. Brossman. A stink bomb in the chemistry classroom." Here she gave a laugh. "Of course, that could have been a student's project gone awry!"

I didn't return the chuckle. I was thinking. "Did this sort of thing go on very long?"

"Oh, no, no. Just a few days. Then it was over, and it's been business as usual ever since. Until now, of course."

I tapped my fingers against my chin. "Was anyone ever caught in regard to this . . . mischief?"

Emily shook her head. "No, I don't believe so. Vandalism seems to have become just an accepted part of our world these days. I don't think the local police put much energy into making an arrest."

"Probably too busy working on the murder to worry over a broken window or two," I suggested, and she shrugged.

"Well, that's a matter open for debate as well, Rose." She shot me a glance, brows arched, smile gone. "But you didn't hear it from me."

When she turned away again, I fired off another question. "What did the local rumor mill have to say? Any ideas?"

"There were those, and, mind you, I wasn't one of

them, who tried to lay the blame on that local Native American group. The one Duncan's with."

"You're kidding! Why?" I rolled my chair a bit closer and sat gazing up at her expectantly.

I think she was sorry she'd spoken. Her shoulders lifted in dismissal, and her answer was vague. "Something to do with that old treaty and how this used to be Indian land. Some folks speculated that they wanted it back and were causing trouble."

"But causing trouble wouldn't get the land back," I pointed out.

Emily tucked her pencil behind her ear and rested her elbows on the top of the ladder. "Exactly what I tried to point out. It was just an excuse to dredge up racial tension, making up bad guys and bogeymen where there were none. Prejudice!" Her lip curled around the word. "That's all it was. No proof, no evidence to point in that direction, but, oh, it made a very convenient explanation."

Leaning back in my chair, I crossed my arms over my chest and pondered. "I hope the problems aren't starting up again."

"That goes double for me, dear. Especially with the celebrations coming up."

"But what would somebody be doing in here so late at night?" I returned to my original topic, thinking out loud. "This room is filled with irreplaceable material, but none of it has any huge monetary value." Pausing for thought, I felt my imagination kick into gear, conjuring up visions of hidden treasures. Maybe a bag of gold coins in one of the filing cabinets. Or an old master hiding behind a not-so-old map, rolled up and stashed somewhere.

Suddenly I remembered Duncan's remark that day in the restaurant about "doing a Nancy Drew," and slapped a hand to my forehead. Despite my denials, I was guilty as charged.

It took effort to draw my attention away from the puzzles of the college and back to the matter at hand. In the past, historical mysteries and what-ifs had more than satisfied my need for intrigue. Since coming to Lunham College, however, I found myself combining the two, until I could see the past melding with the present, creating a link between both times that outweighed the draw of the separate parts.

It was that link, I'm sure of it, which led me to the chapel after work that night. The Bible had been duly installed in its glass case after the O'Briens' presentation, and I longed to take a good look at it. I was also aching for a closer examination of the chapel itself, after doing all that reading on its construction. So, after an uninspired dinner in the commons—salad, mixed vegetables, and pasta—I made my way to the tunnels.

I wouldn't even have attempted the lonely walk underground if it weren't for the weather. The wind was blowing briskly from the north, accompanied by an early dose of freezing rain that merely hinted at the long winter to come.

The tunnel, I noticed as I entered, smelled musty and damp. Bits of trodden leaves indicated others had recently passed this way, and the concrete floor was spotted with tiny puddles, slow to evaporate in the enclosed space. I set off at a brisk pace, head up, shoulders back, confident and purposeful. Halfway along, however, I couldn't resist the urge to glance over my shoulder. Indistinguishable sounds seemed to come from behind—the slow drip of a leak somewhere overhead, the scurrying noise that could be those dried leaves caught in a draft or something small and furry. Nothing revealed itself to my anxious gaze, and I stepped up to a trot. Just when I'd begun to think I'd never reach the end and had started to feel claustrophobic, the door to the chapel appeared.

I scrambled up the steps to ground level and pushed open the heavy door at the top. A glance around showed me I was in the foyer of the building. It was an unheated space about ten feet square. To my right was the big double door leading outside; to my left, the chapel itself. I headed left.

Like all places of worship, the chapel was hushed. There were no other occupants, I noticed at once and was glad.

The chapel was small. Less than a dozen rows of pews stretched on either side of the main aisle. Under my hand the elaborately carved wood was smooth and cool. Slowly I walked down the aisle, turning to look at the legendary stained-glass windows I'd read so much about. It was late afternoon and, without sunshine, the windows were darkened and difficult to distinguish at a distance. With their muted colors in detailed depictions of Biblical scenes, the windows would be stunning when softly, gently illuminated.

Moving slowly, I went closer for a better look, tipping my head to gaze up at the intricate patterns, marveling at the hours of workmanship each window represented. How long had it taken to create the lifelike flow of an angel's robe? How many shades of red had been used to bring out the texture and depth of the cloth? There were six windows in all, and I took my time admiring each of them, working my way to the front of the chapel.

I lingered a bit over the memorial plaques, noticing the still-bright one honoring the murdered board member, Samuel Felber. How come every time that man came to mind, I was in a potentially frightening place? I wondered as I stood alone in the quiet, darkened chapel while the rain slashed just outside.

Off to one side of the deceptively simple marble altar, the old Bible was on display, and I eagerly stepped over to examine it. It had been placed in a glass-topped wooden case. A big brass lock at the front looked more decorative than sturdy, and I gave the lid a tug, but the lock held fast. Attached to the back of the cabinet was an oblong reading lamp on a flexible metal coil. I switched it on, splashing golden light across the fragile, brittle-looking pages of the book under glass.

The Bible had been opened to a particularly dazzling page of illumination, with the jeweled ribbon marker displayed down the center. The two items competed in their brilliance, the jewellike colors on the paper a reflection of the sparkling gems.

I clasped my hands behind my back and leaned over the case, eliminating the glare of the lamp against the glass. After a moment my hand came around to the glass, and I trailed a finger above the ribbon, wishing I could touch the jewels themselves. Something about the clear, bright colors of gemstones always reminded me of candy. Like the jelly beans I eagerly consumed as a child, they gleamed and glowed with every color of the rainbow.

Lunham College may have been able to make more immediate use of a gift of cash, but this historical legacy was certainly more enduring.

Through the heavy brick walls, I caught the whistle of the wind outside, and my gaze swept to the windows. The trees beyond cast shifting shadows, barely discernible as twilight took hold.

I should really head for home, I knew. My work was done for the day. I'd seen the Bible in all its glory. It was time to return to my quiet apartment. The television could be my company, and I had something frozen in the refrigerator for dinner. I grimaced, turning away from the Bible and snapping off the reading light. The prospect of home wasn't welcoming, and I felt the familiar itch beginning in my feet.

Not now! Not so soon! I thought, fighting the rise of panic. I'd barely settled in to the place and the job. I didn't want to succumb to the trapped feeling I'd gotten so often in the past. Too often.

I could hear myself breathing, raspy and shallow, and closed my eyes, counting slowly to ten, then twenty. *Actually,* I thought with a wry smile, *I couldn't be in a better place for this self-induced crisis.* The sense of peace and calm could fill me up, if I let it.

Slipping into a pew about halfway back, directly under a frosted lantern on a heavy silver chain, I sat heavily, my hands supporting me on each side. For a long while I tried to keep my mind blank, until, at last, I felt up to the confrontation I faced.

All my life I'd been running. Moving so often as a child had made me unable to stay in one place for long. Even, like now, when I truly wanted to stay, when I had good reasons to be optimistic about the future. It began with this itchy, restless feeling that nagged at me in ever-increasing degrees. And ended with hasty farewells and no explanations, leaving behind confusion and hard feelings and, just occasionally, broken hearts.

The last time had been the worst. I thought I really loved Steve. I had told myself I did. I'd even managed to convince myself I could live happily ever after in the scenic village of Tumble Creek, married to an insurance man. The American dream, mine for the taking.

I looked at my hands, twisted together in my lap, and remembered the sparkle of Steve's engagement ring on my finger. That image was followed almost immediately by another—Steve's face when I called it off. The hurt in his eyes still haunted me, even though over a year had passed. His voice, bitter with disappointment, echoed in my ears.

"It's because you were an Army brat!" he said in anger. "You'll never be able to stay in one place, never be happy unless you know you can pick up and run. Well, then, go ahead and run, Rose. Keep chasing your rainbow. I really hope you catch it, but I don't think you ever will."

Condemned. I felt condemned to a life of flight. But from what? Drudgery? Routine? Sameness? Life at Lunham College had been anything but routine, so far. With Duncan around, drudgery didn't seem like a possibility, either. In fact, with Duncan around, life was very promising. I liked him. I liked his kisses. His intelligence was admirable, his dedication quite commendable. That fiery spark in his eyes guaranteed life would never be dull.

I smiled as I pictured him, debating a point, defending his opinion, moving closer for a kiss. The itch in my feet receded, fading slowly away one toe at a time, and the calm I had sought took its place. I sat on in the darkness, the wooden pew hard against my back, and felt that calm spread through my body. When my eyes closed, I made no attempt to open them. When sleep came, I drifted off easily, the wind outside and the patter of the raindrops forming a perfect lullaby.

The tinkle of glass woke me, sounding on the edge of my consciousness and registering slowly. Blinking, I looked around me, unsure of my surroundings. My eyes roamed around, trying to place what I saw in some sort of context. Above me, I could see a vaulted ceiling, inlaid with mosaics of some kind. Below these, on the walls, I was just able to distinguish the outline of windows. Seeing them, memory returned, and I realized I'd fallen sound asleep in the dark chapel. As I dozed, I'd slumped over, my head resting on the back of the pew. I was about to move, to push myself upright, when a sound from the altar froze me.

The sound of broken glass being brushed aside was like chimes in the quiet chapel. The noise was the same as the one that had awakened me, and it took only an instant to conclude someone was breaking into the place of worship.

Soundlessly I slipped off the pew to the cold stone floor. The disturbance had been up front. If whoever was there looked out over the pews, I didn't want them to see me. Holding my breath, my body tensed in every muscle, I strained to hear. Muffled movement, the occasional grinding sound of glass being crushed under a heavy shoe, the rise and fall of someone breathing. From outside, the wail of the wind had increased, and freezing rain pelted the windows with increasing force.

I'm not one for praying. I always figured God did His part just creating me and I was pretty much on my own from there. But I prayed now, silently, repetitively, using the words to keep from jumping up and running. My fingers were clenched into hot, tight fists, curled at my sides, and the echo of my heart thumped in my ears.

The prayer must have worked—to some extent, anyway. Within minutes, logic returned to my frightened brain, easing my fear and replacing it with something that could have been more dangerous—curiosity.

Still on my knees, I straightened up slowly, my hands gripping the back of the pew just in front. An inch at a time, I rose higher until just my eyes peeked over the wooden panel, like Kilroy. At first I couldn't see any life forms. The altar area was pitch black in the night. Then, off to one side, I saw a spot of light, bobbing about, playing over the display case containing the old Bible.

Of course! Someone was planning to steal the antique. It was said to be worth a fortune. The jeweled bookmark worth even more! I almost gasped at the realization, biting back the breath just in time.

Frantically I searched for a way to stop the burglar. I couldn't just sit here, hiding like a mouse, and allow the ancient artifact to be heisted. But what could I do? I had no weapon, no means to threaten the prowler or defend myself.

While I squatted, watching and thinking, I made out the dark form of a person holding the bobbing flashlight.

Just like in the movies, the would-be thief was dressed from head to toe in dark colors. If it was a man, he was no taller than I, slightly built, almost skinny. His face was obscured by some sort of covering, and I cursed under my breath. Identifying the intruder would be impossible.

He moved without hesitation, pausing for only a moment to shine his light on the display case before taking the end of the flashlight and bringing it down heavily against the glass. It shattered and I flinched, my eyes squeezing shut until the sound faded.

A gloved hand reached inside the box. I could picture it closing over the fragile book binding, wrenching the centuries-old Bible from the protective case and spiriting it away. If the rain fell on it, if it were dropped and torn. . . .

The archivist in me shrank from the image and spurred me into foolhardy action. Yanking off my shoe, I rose in a flash. Just before I flung the pump in the direction of the burglar's head, I shouted, "Hey! You!"

Hurling the object with all my might, I was glad the distance between us wasn't farther.

Startled, the burglar looked up, raising his arms over his face to ward off the coming blow. The shoe bounced against his shoulder and clattered to the floor. He didn't stop to see if I'd follow my attack with another missile, but spun on his heel and disappeared into the shadows on the side of the altar.

I slipped out of the remaining shoe and, holding it in my hand, scurried up the aisle. One glance at the display case revealed that, despite my efforts, damage had been done.

The Bible remained, tilted at an angle on a bed of broken glass. But the jeweled marker no longer draped across the pages. So easy to clutch in a fist. So portable. Too portable. The priceless ribbon had been taken from the center of the book. The small fortune in gemstones was gone.

It's difficult to know how you'll react in an emergency, what you'll do when faced with an unusual and imperative dilemma. I did the only thing I could think and retrieved my far-flung shoe, stuffed my foot into it, and made a mad dash for the tunnel back to the main building.

The thief was gone. There was no sense pursuing him. Since the chapel was tucked in the woods, the idea of returning via the outdoors put me off. For one, the criminal was out there, in those same woods. Also, the rain still fell and, in the darkness, I could easily lose my way.

Down the stairs I clamored, my feet landing heavily on each step. The adrenaline racing through my blood, edged with fear, gave me more strength than usual, and I wrenched open the door to the tunnel with such force it slammed back against the wall. By the time it shut behind me, I was a good fifty feet down the dim passageway, running flat-out and gasping.

Usually the trip back from just about anywhere seems shorter than the trip there. Not this time. It seemed as if I ran a mile, fighting the stitch in my side and trying not to imagine demons coming up behind me. Demons waving faded pink ribbons encrusted with jewels.

At last, just as necessity slowed my steps, the door to the main building appeared, and I rushed through. Within minutes I was pelting down the main corridor of the college, my footsteps ringing noisily in the deserted hallway, heading for the information booth and the telephone that sat there.

No one was on duty now, so late in the day, and I scooted around the countertop, collapsing in the desk chair. Pressing one hand against my chest, I forced myself to take a few deep, calming breaths before dialing. My fingers still shook as I punched the numbers. 9-1-1.

The next call I placed was to Duncan. He answered on the first ring, as if he were expecting the call, but the surprise in his voice at my news was quite genuine.

"Where are you now?" he asked urgently. After I told him, he ordered, "Stay right there. I'll be over in ten minutes. You're supposed to meet the police at the chapel?"

"No, no." I shook my head. "They're meeting me here, at the front entrance, so I can lead the way to the chapel," I explained.

"I'd better hurry then." The phone went dead against my ear, and I hung it up slowly.

Leaning back in the chair, I crossed my arms over my chest and shivered with nervous reaction. Even as I did so, I could hear the far-off wail of a police siren, sounding lonely and forlorn in the night. I pressed my eyes closed and sighed. It was going to be a very long night.

Duncan and I stood at the back of the chapel, watching as several police officers roamed the altar area, taking notes and photographs. The quiet sanctuary had been turned into a hub of activity, and I was happy to have Duncan beside me while I waited to see if I was still needed.

I'd told my story about the burglary to the two officers who had arrived in a screech of tires. They'd radioed for a few others to help with the investigation, and once the backups had appeared, we'd all used the tunnel to cross to the chapel.

Duncan had shown up just as the expedition set off, greeting me with a warm hug of support. For the first time in hours I relaxed, soaking in the feeling of his embrace.

As we'd navigated the underground path, I repeated my story for Duncan's benefit. At one point the officer on my right interrupted. Pointing at Duncan, he said, "You look very familiar."

In the dim light I thought I saw Duncan color as he quipped, "Well, I haven't been arrested lately."

"No," the officer pursued the issue. "I think it was. . . . Yes, that protest. That Indian thing."

Duncan sighed. "Very good, Officer. I was at 'that Indian thing.' And we were peaceful and respectful, which is more than I can say for the opposition." He gave his eyes a dramatic roll, then encouraged me to finish telling my tale.

When I got to the point of my confrontation with the burglar, Duncan stopped short and pulled me against him, murmuring, "What are you, crazy?" in a tender tone. Worry lines appeared on either side of his mouth, punctuating his concern. With a stubble of beard making shadows on his cheeks, he looked more handsome than ever. In his haste he'd neglected to bring his fake glasses, so his eyes stood out, not hidden by glare. Gazing into them, I felt a tingle from another kind of excitement crawl up my spine and did my best to ignore the inappropriate physical response rushing through me.

"I'm fine now," I assured him, rubbing my hands up and down his forearms. The nubby material of his worn jacket was soft under my hands, and I concentrated on that sensual pleasure, blocking out the reason for his presence here.

After a moment one of the officers cleared his throat loudly, suggesting, "Perhaps we should move on."

His voice penetrated, as it was meant to, and I flushed, smiling sheepishly.

Once we reached the crime site, the professionals sprang into action, leaving Duncan and me to our own devices. For the most part, we sat silently side by side. Duncan kept a firm clasp on my hand, his thumb moving in an endless circle against my palm.

"Wait until Brossman hears about this," he said at last. "First the murder. Now a theft. And the display case didn't even have time to get dusty!"

At the thought of Dr. Brossman, I frowned. We'd had a hasty introduction in the hallway outside his office one day a week ago, when Lily and I had been meeting for a luncheon date. Lily did the honors with her usual casual flair, and the college president had barely broken stride to pump my hand before hurrying off. Our meeting had been an interruption to him.

And now I was about to cause him more trouble as the messenger of really bad news.

Duncan laughed out loud at my stricken look, the sound filling this solemn place in a way that seemed wholly inappropriate. My eyes widened, and I pursed my lips, glancing to the altar, where a few of the policemen had looked up from their tasks. His chuckle dropped off instantly, ending with a sigh as Duncan shifted on the hard wooden seat beside me.

"Rose," he said, giving me a comical chuck under the chin, "it isn't your fault the theft took place. Brossman will hardly hold you responsible. If anything, he'll give you a bonus for being a hero!"

"What?"

"Well, it was your quick thinking that hurried the thief away. If you hadn't beaned him with your shoe, he'd have made off with the Bible too."

"Hmm." I tapped my chin, then smiled, thanking him for the reassuring words by giving his hand a tight squeeze. "That's one way to look at it," I admitted. "I just hope Brossman sees the situation your way." Rolling my eyes at this latest dilemma, I wished for a moment that I'd chosen any other time to pay my first visit to the chapel. I like excitement as much as the next person, but enough was enough.

"You know, it was rather foolhardy to confront that burglar," Duncan reprimanded, sliding his arm up and around my shoulders. "If he had a weapon, you could have gotten injured. Or worse."

Another angle I hadn't considered and one that chilled me straight through in retrospect.

"Right again," I admitted. I hesitated just an instant before relaxing against the warmth of Duncan's body. When I wiggled my toes, they didn't itch at all. I thought, *That's a good sign.*

When Dr. Brossman appeared half an hour later, his agitated strides carried him down the aisle and past us to the officer who was directing the investigation. We watched as he nervously listened to the details of the theft, jangling the change in his pockets and fidgeting from one foot to the other. This was not a happy man.

At one point, the officer turned and gestured in my direction. Brossman narrowed his eyes as he looked my way, but I put that down to the fact that his glasses were stored in the top pocket of his coat and not on his nose. He was just squinting to get a look at me. I was sure of it.

After their conversation had ended, the president thanked the officer and headed back up the aisle toward us.

Duncan removed his arm from around me and rose, greeting him with the words, "Quite a blow for the school, Dr. Brossman. Do the police have any leads?"

The heavyset man was fishing in his pocket for a package of cigarettes and took the time to light one, blowing a cloud of noxious fumes heavenward before replying. "A blow, yes. Certainly a blow." He shook his head. "Damaging for us, of course. Just have to hope they catch the bugger." His eyes, lost in shadows and the bulge of his own cheeks, shot to me, and I swallowed hard.

"Good work, Claypool. Guess the school owes you great thanks. Lucky thing you were here. Brave of you."

I gave a sigh of relief, letting my breath out in a whoosh. "Thank you, sir. I only wish the ribbon had been saved as well."

Heavy shoulders lifted in a shrug that strained the seams of his coat. "Couldn't be helped." Another drag on the cigarette. Another toxic cloud overhead. "I do wish you would have phoned me first. Rather have heard it directly from you than from the police. Puts me at a disadvantage this way."

I nodded agreement, although I really didn't understand the distinction. "I guess I wasn't thinking straight. It would have been simple to call you." I attempted a joke. "I'm not used to being part of a crime. I don't know the standard procedure."

The joke went over his head, however. "No reason you should." He looked away, back at the police, frowning at something. "Excuse me." He strutted away like a man on a mission, chest thrust forward, arms swinging.

Duncan and I sat down again.

"Does he always speak in incomplete sentences?" I asked, wrinkling my nose.

"Yes," Duncan said, nodding and grinning. "You can use it as a barometer of his mood, actually. The more upset he is, the shorter his sentences become. Some staff meetings, he just stammers out single words. If it weren't so irritating, it would almost be laughable. The man's a coronary just waiting to happen," he went on, sobering.

Dr. Brossman definitely seemed like a type-A person now, blustering and intruding as the policemen worked around him.

I blinked heavily, my eyes feeling droopy and gritty. "How much longer do I have to stay here?" I asked Duncan, just a hint of whine in my voice.

He shot out an arm, glanced at his watch, and shrugged. "If the cops know where to find you, I'd think it's safe to leave. You wait there, and I'll check with the chief."

Gratefully remaining seated, I watched as he sought out the officer, held a brief conversation, and returned to my side.

"No problem, Rose. Let's go." He held out a hand, and I took it, letting him pull me to my feet.

Our journey through the tunnel was a slow one, the gray walls reflecting my own lack of energy.

"If I never see this tunnel again, it will be too soon," I told Duncan with a weak smile. "I think I've crossed it half a dozen times in the last three hours!"

Duncan's arm at my waist squeezed me tight, and he slowed his step to plant a kiss at my temple. I closed my eyes, leaning into him, bringing my feet to a standstill. It was really a rather romantic setting—the deserted tunnel, the dim light, the late hour.

Wordlessly I turned to face him and reached up to stroke his cheek. My eyes scanned his features, moving from his soulful, sparkling eyes to the hollow of his throat, to the scattered silver hairs highlighting his temples.

"Duncan, thanks for coming tonight and being with me," I whispered, my fingers twining into the long locks on the top of his head. "It would have been a nightmare without you."

One corner of his mouth tipped up, dimpling a cheek. "I hope I'll always bring you pleasant dreams, Rose. No nightmares ever."

I couldn't wait any longer for the feel of those soft lips and urged him closer. He didn't put up any fuss, but accepted my invitation.

Our lips matched perfectly, fitting together like the pieces of a puzzle. His were warm, smooth, and stirring.

I slid my arms around his neck, and he nestled tight against me. His legs pressed on mine, his hand at the back of my waist drawing me closer still. The tingle I felt in my toes now had nothing to do with the urge to travel or make good an escape and everything to do with this wonderful man I had found. Considerate, thoughtful, and inspired, he seemed too good to be true. But I wasn't dreaming; this was blissful reality.

"Oh, Rose," he whispered against my parted lips. "Sweet Rose."

Once more my eyes danced closed, and the ground fell away beneath my feet.

Chapter Nine

There isn't a place on earth where news gets around faster than in a small town. By the time I arrived at school the next morning, the entire staff was already abuzz, and several reporters were waiting near the archives door in a knot, anxious to talk to me.

My heart, which had been light and filled, remarkably, with song, plummeted to my ankles, and my hand tightened around the handle of my purse. I didn't relish the personal publicity this incident would bring or the time away from my job it would entail.

Standing in the corridor, I held court as briefly as possible, telling the newspeople what had happened and where, then directing them to Dr. Brossman with the rest of their questions. When they pressed further, I adopted a politician's stance, shaking my head as I pushed through the tangle of bodies and repeating over and over, "You'll have to ask Dr. Brossman. You'll have to check with the president."

The archives door opened as I turned the key, and I

made quick work of slipping inside, sending an apologetic smile over my shoulder. I leaned against the door, listening as the reporters' voices and footsteps faded away, then turned my attention to the job at hand.

My only interruption was a welcome one from Lily, bringing me coffee and a doughnut and about a thousand questions. It was an hour or more before her curiosity was satisfied. I worked as I talked while she sat on the side of my desk, swinging one leg.

"I'll tell you, things have certainly livened up around here since you came," she told me, getting up to leave.

Reassuring news, I thought.

At noon I rang Duncan's office and asked him to stop by. I'd been setting aside items that would suit the historical displays he was planning, and the cardboard box I'd put them in was full. He arranged to come over after his last class of the day, around four o'clock.

Another thing I enjoy about my job is the opportunity to work on my own, undisturbed. That's what happened that day, except for the three hours when Karen joined me to work on the wall mural. I made a few conversational forays, directing them at her back as she perched on the ladder and painted.

I wanted to ask her about that speeding car in the woods. I hadn't forgotten her yellow scarf, and although the idea that she was the passenger in the car that nearly hit Duncan and me was tenuous at best, it was the only idea I had. After a few exchanges of chitchat, she began to thaw a little, and we shared a few observations about the school and some of the instructors.

Eventually I said, "You know, I thought I saw you the other day in the woods."

Her brush hesitated, then resumed. "Really? Where?"

"Near the service road. I was out walking, and this big car shot by." I shrugged. "I thought it was you."

"Yes. You were right. I was with my boyfriend, actually." She gave a derisive snort of laughter. "We were having a fight, and when he's angry, he drives like a nut. One time I got out at a stoplight and walked home! He's so stubborn!" She sounded annoyed and disgusted.

"I think they're all that way," I commiserated, nodding.

"Well, it's very aggravating." Karen sighed, and it was like a door opening. I was an ear to listen, a sounding board, and she took the opportunity to unburden herself.

It wasn't a very complicated story or an unusual one. He took her for granted. Didn't call when he said he would, forgot plans they made.

"And lately he's been so distracted." Again the brush paused. "I wonder if there's somebody else?"

The eternal question. I tried to be reassuring. "There probably isn't, Karen. It's probably something else entirely. Trouble at work or maybe it's a money crunch. Just ask him," I suggested.

She nodded. "I suppose I should." When she looked at me, she was smiling. "Aren't men complicated?" she asked.

That question didn't need an answer. We both just laughed.

By the time Duncan appeared, about twenty after four, Karen was long gone. He looked harried and breathless, puffing, "Sorry I'm late, Rose. I got tied up with Georgia again." His eyebrows shot up, and his cheeks flushed as he stated, "That woman drives me crazy!"

For the second time that day, my heart sank a little. Aiming for a nonchalant tone and still working with the photo I held, I said, "Oh? Why is that?"

"Why is that?" Duncan echoed, coming to stand behind me and rubbing my shoulders with a firm, warm grip. It felt heavenly, and I tipped my head to each side as he massaged the tension out of my body. "I'll tell you why! Her views on the political foundations of this country and its future are incredibly outdated! Great change is needed if we're to progress with the next century!" As his fervor grew, so did the strength of his grip, and by the end of his tirade, I was wincing in pain.

"Duncan, Duncan, stop!" I gasped, dropping the photograph onto my desk and making a grab at his hands. "You're hurting me!"

"What?" It took a moment for my words to penetrate the cloud of aggravation circling around him. "Oh, sorry!" He released me with a gentle pat and shook his head. "I get irate sometimes, you know."

"I hadn't noticed," I joked, rubbing the sore spots.

He grimaced, moving from me to the carton I'd set aside earlier. Even as he dipped into the box of papers and artifacts I'd marked for his perusal, he muttered under his breath about the problematic Georgia.

I made noises of sympathy, but inside I felt relieved. Apparently, to Duncan's way of thinking, there seemed to be no attraction between the two. Of course, he hadn't seen the way Georgia watched him at the reception. He hadn't seen the look in her eyes. Was he aware, I wondered, of the direction her thoughts were taking?

"Hey!" Duncan's exclamation drew my attention back to the present. He'd been carefully lifting out the items in the box, examining them to judge their suitability for the display. Now he held a fragile, yellowed sheaf of papers that I had placed in an acid-free envelope and waved them enthusiastically. "Where on earth did you ever find this? Is it an original? It looks old enough." He ran his hand over the envelope as if it could answer his questions.

I squinted, trying to recall what that particular envelope held. After a few moments memory served, and I tapped the envelope with my finger. "It's the oddest thing, Duncan. One of the cabinet drawers I was going through had a bunch of old books at the back. Nothing valuable. Nothing even memorable, actually. Just junk. Before I sent them on the way to the dustbin, I put them in an old box, and when I lifted it, the bottom fell out. The books took a tumble and, being so old, a few of the bindings ripped."

Duncan nodded when I paused for breath. His cheeks were flushed pink with excitement, and he prodded me on. "And . . . and. . . ."

"And when I picked them up, that fell out from under the leather cover on one of those tattered old books." Stabbing a finger at the papers he held, I shrugged. "How they ever got there—or why—I have no idea. It was a very hazardous place to house such an important document."

"You've read it then?" Duncan asked, slipping the papers carefully from the envelope.

"Well, no," I told him. "I only came across it this afternoon. I just looked at the title page. It says it's the treaty between the Indians and old man Lunham, deeding over this land for the college. But if it is, what's it doing here? And how did it end up inside an old book?"

Duncan fingered the edge of the paper, yellowed and cracked, putting it down when I scowled in disapproval. "Yes, that's awfully odd."

I nodded. "Too odd."

"Well, it would have to be authenticated, of course. And if it's genuine, it would be quite a plum for the centennial display. I'd like to make a photocopy of this, if you don't mind. I promise you I'll be very careful with the pages, and I'll be back in five minutes. I won't even stop to talk to anyone in the corridor," he added, holding out both hands as he pleaded.

"Nothing doing," I stated. "If it's real, it will be micro-filmed immediately, along with all these other items. And if it's fake—well, then it's worthless, and you can burn it in your fireplace. But until the matter is proven one way or the other, it's going in the school safe."

Duncan looked crestfallen. His lower lip protruded the tiniest bit, and his scowl emphasized his disappointment. "Okay, Rose. You're the boss," he conceded with good grace. "Would it be all right if I read it over and took some notes?" If there was sarcasm in his request, I chose to overlook it.

"Of course you can. But you'll have to wear these." I tossed him a pair of my plain cotton gloves and watched with some amusement as he tried to fit his big hands into them.

Flexing his fingers and grimacing, he said, "This is awful! I think I'm cutting off the circulation."

Pulling a chair over for him, I said with a chuckle, "Then you'd better read fast!"

Half an hour later as I cleaned off my work brushes and tidied up, Duncan gave a shout that made me jump. "Rose! I think I've found something special here. Look at this!"

Rag in hand, I crossed to where Duncan perched, the pages of the document spread out on the tabletop before him. "What is it?"

He turned to look up at me, eyes shining with excitement. His voice reflected it, too, coming fast and furious as I struggled to take it all in. "I've examined the copy of this treaty that's in Brossman's office. First, just out of my own curiosity, but then again when I became involved with the Native American group. That copy ends right here." He pointed at a page filled with faded, crabbed writing. At the bottom were half a dozen signatures and about as many big black X's, indicating the legal signatures of the tribe's leaders.

"Then, what's this page?" I asked, gesturing with my rag at the piece of paper just to the left.

"Good question," Duncan said, leaning over the old document. " 'Special provision for the family of Chief White Star and his descendants,' " he read slowly, struggling to decipher the faded words.

" 'It is agreed between the parties that the following portion of land will be held in reservation for the chief and his descendants, as he claims in his own right and with full power and authority to sell or dispose of same.

Namely, beginning at the shore of the lake at a point eleven chains above the—' " He broke off here as the document continued to detail longitude and latitude.

Duncan sat back, hands resting heavily on his thighs, and commented, "Huh. What do you think of that?"

I shook my head, then reread the passage. We exchanged a look of professional appraisal, and I saw a glimmer of hope in his eye. A historian looking at a possible find, I knew part of him was eager to accept the paper at face value, but, intellectually, he knew he couldn't. And neither could I.

I said, "I don't buy it. A page you've never seen before, meaning what?"

"Well, according to this page, it looks as if some of this college could be built on land that technically still belongs to the chief's descendants."

I remembered the headlines so prevalent in the newspapers these days—enforcing old treaties, reclaiming land and hunting rights.

"Awfully convenient, turning up now." I shifted my weight and sighed. "If a member of this chief's family survived and this piece of paper existed then, it would have been presented and acted upon ages ago!"

Duncan nodded. "You'd certainly think so." He leaned over the paper, nose nearly touching the print. "If it is a fake, it's a darn good one. This ink, the texture, the color. I wonder. . . ."

"What? You wonder what?"

He straightened up. "Assuming it's a forgery, and I think that's what we both believe, who created it and when? The why seems obvious."

"To get access to the college's land," I supplied, and

he nodded. "And how did it end up in here? Look around, Duncan! I'm making headway on this room, but it could have been months before I found it—and it may have been here for years before I came. The record keeping in here was nonexistent, you know."

"True enough," Duncan conceded, drumming his fingers on the edge of the table, and I wondered what he was thinking now to cloud his brow so.

"Dr. Brossman will have to be told at once," I went on, "even if it turns out to be a forgery. He should be informed of this discovery."

Duncan gave a snort. "I'm glad that isn't my job." He looked at me over his shoulder as he carefully restacked the pages of the treaty and returned them to their envelope. "You going to tell him now?"

One glance at the clock showed me that would be impossible, and I shook my head. Taking the envelope and its precious cargo from Duncan, I said, "It's waited all this while. Another few hours won't make much difference, I guess."

Duncan stood up, stretching his hands over his head. "Hey, don't look so glum. No use borrowing trouble. And in any event, it hardly concerns you."

I sighed, my eyes straying to the partially completed mural slowly spreading across the opposite wall. "It's coming along nicely, isn't it?" I digressed, gesturing at the painting, and Duncan nodded in admiration.

"I know you're right, Duncan, and I promise not to lose sleep over this. It's just one more puzzle to solve around here, after all. I guess I just hate having to approach Dr. Brossman again. If this is a fake, it's meaningless, and I'm wasting his time. If it's genuine, the school could be in real trouble, and I'll be the bearer of bad news. Again." When I scowled, I furrowed my brow and pressed my lips together tight.

"Just turn on the charm," Duncan quipped, giving me a saucy wink. "Sure works on me." He stepped closer, one hand reaching out to capture mine.

I fought back a smile for about two seconds, then let it spill forth as I tugged him close. I hadn't had much time for thinking since last night, since Duncan had acted as a tower of support through the long ordeal of the police investigation. It wasn't that I was trying to avoid confronting my growing feelings for this man. How could I possibly reconcile them with my long-standing history of bolting at regular intervals? That was a puzzle I didn't want to tackle, I'll admit. But tackle it I would, as soon as a free moment presented itself.

Maybe tonight, I thought as I closed my eyes for Duncan's kiss. *In a warm bubble bath. . . .*

But my bath was not to come for hours and hours that night. First, we had a meeting to attend.

Duncan's battered old car chugged down the road, laboring heavily with the effort. I fingered a hole in the side of the passenger door and shook my head.

"You know, this is a jagged hunk of plastic, Duncan. I could get a cut from this," I scolded.

He took his eyes off the road long enough to see what I was talking about, then said, "Well, take your finger out of there, Rose."

I wrinkled my nose at such obvious logic, wondering if he always approached problems in such a clearheaded but simplistic way. He didn't give me much time to ponder.

"You're going to love Peter, Rose," he said, checking the mirror before changing lanes. "He's so energetic and focused. He's the leader of this group, but he also relies heavily on input from the rest of us. It's a real democracy, this organization, which is ironic when you think about it. About the group challenging government offices set up by another democracy."

I nodded. In my lap I held Duncan's notes about the old treaty. In the hands of a well-organized go-getter, they could be the fuse to a powder keg. It was sure to be an interesting evening.

The drive to the big office building where the group met didn't take very long, and soon we were pulling into the parking lot. Plenty of people were working late. The lot was well over half full, and lights were on in many of the office windows.

As Duncan struggled to get the car into a tight spot, I scanned the other automobiles nearby, noticing the red sticker they all sported on their rear bumpers.

When Duncan shut off the engine, the silence made my ears ring. He jangled his keys. "Don't open the door. I'll come around." Quickly he circled the car and wrestled open the door, waving me out.

Clutching the papers in one hand and my purse in the other, I fell into step beside him. We'd only gone about thirty feet—he talking, me listening—before I stopped dead in my tracks. My feet scuffed the asphalt, sending pebbles sailing, and my mouth dropped open.

"Duncan, look." I pointed at the car in front of us. More specifically, I indicated the rear bumper of the big black automobile. It sported a yellow government license plate and a red sticker.

"What?" He looked at the car, at me, back to the car. "What?"

"This is the car that nearly ran us over that day in the woods!" I said, realizing the truth of it as I formed the words. I jumped up and down a little, feeling shaky with a mixture of excitement and remembered fear.

I ran around to the driver's side and pressed my nose against the window. The interior needed a vacuum. The ashtray overflowed, and the window was foggy with smoke residue.

"Yech!" I groaned.

"How can you possibly tell if this is the same car that nearly ran us over?" Duncan's voice was tinged with impatience, and when I looked over at him, I saw his eyes stray to the lighted office windows.

He must be afraid we'll be late or something, I thought, a little impatient myself.

Straightening up, I said in all honesty, "It's just a feeling I've got. If you can believe that. I just. . . ." I gestured vaguely before concluding, "I just know!" I wasn't about to utter that clichéd phrase, "women's intuition," but from the look on Duncan's face, I may as well have.

He gave his eyes a roll, knowing full well I'd see it. "You'll forgive me if I'm unconvinced, Rose. But I'd like to point out there must be at least a dozen black cars with government plates and parking stickers in this lot." He swept a hand to indicate the vast space of asphalt surrounding us. "This is a government office building, after all, and you do need a sticker to park in this lot."

I shrugged and moved past him. "You could be right," I told him. "The things you say make sense. But I know this is the car, and I think we should see who gets in and drives it away."

"We have a meeting to attend, an important one. We don't have time to launch some sort of stakeout!"

Pursing my lips, I thought for a moment and reached a compromise I could live with. "I'm sitting near the window at this meeting, Duncan. So I can keep an eye on this car." I jabbed a finger in the direction of it as Duncan started wagging his head in disbelief.

"From twelve floors up and in the dark. Good luck, Rose."

I hate to be wrong, and I'll rarely admit it when I am. It's one of my biggest faults. But this time there was no denying it. From the best seat in the house overlooking the parking lot with truly a bird's-eye view, there was no way to actually effectively watch that car. I had a hard time locating it, first of all, from the altered perspective. Then, as twilight deepened and the lot's overhead lights blinked on feebly, the area filled with shadows and patches of darkness. And, lastly, the conversation at the meeting was so intriguing, I kept forgetting to glance out the window. After an hour or so I gave up entirely, devoting my attention solely to the discussion taking place around me.

Peter Moore, the group's official leader, wasn't in attendance just yet. Working late was the official explanation, and the members of the group all chuckled since it was well known his office was just down the hall in the city clerk's office.

Karen and I sat next to each other. Since we'd shared our views on the male of the species, we seemed to have forged a bond. When Duncan and I had entered the room tonight, she'd patted the seat beside her and greeted me with a broad smile. During the meeting I noticed her taking plenty of notes and guessed she was the secretary of the group.

About an hour into the meeting, the group took a break. Everyone stood, stretching. Some folks wandered out into the hall and down to the soda machine in the staff lounge.

While Duncan chatted with Karen, the only person in the room familiar to me, I moved to the window and gazed down into the lot. At first all I could see was my own reflection in the glass. Eventually, though, I made out the big black car sitting silent and deserted in the lot far below.

I sighed, wishing Duncan would believe me when I said that was the car. I wished I had more evidence to support my claim than just this nebulous sense of certainty. The hub of conversation continued behind me. Resting my forehead against the cool pane of glass, I thought about that car with its overflowing ashtray. That car, on college property for a reason as yet unknown.

Then, prickling at the edge of my brain, another thought intruded. Memory, actually. The memory of the archives late one night, when a cigarette smoldered dangerously in the trash bin.

Maybe I read too many novels or watch too much late-night television, but suddenly I saw a connection. I lifted my head off the glass, my hands gripping the sill tightly, as if trying to grasp this hazy trail from A to B before it evaporated.

Could it have been the driver of the car who was in the archives that night? Why? What would his purpose have been?

Behind me, I heard Duncan chuckle and remembered our big discovery.

Why would an important legal document be hidden away like that if, in fact, the document was bonafide?

I bit my lower lip and asked the question on the flip side. If it was a forgery, who executed it? And when? How had it ended up in the archives? My archives?

My breath came out on a sigh. I hadn't forgotten the note I'd received telling me to leave well enough alone. Someone warning me away. Afraid I'd find the treaty? Perhaps. Then again, I knew a person had been in the place, late at night—and left their cigarette burning there. The same someone, looking for the document?

Who? Who? The words echoed in my brain like the call of the wild as I wondered who could be looking for the paper and what they hoped to gain by finding it. Again, so much depended on the integrity of the document.

If it were declared valid, the descendants of Chief White Star could gain substantially, while the college became the big loser. Maybe my intruder was a family member, eager to claim his inheritance. Maybe it was a faculty member, just as eager to protect the school and his position in it.

Hmm. I pictured Dr. Brossman creeping down a dark corridor, crazy Harriet trailing helpfully behind with a flashlight. The vision was ridiculous. While the others in the room continued their conversations, I brainstormed on the mystery.

My fingers itched to get at paper and pencil so I could make some notes and draw a map connecting my various mental clues. As interesting as I found this meeting and the group's plans to retrieve artifacts from the museum, right now I was more intrigued by the drama closer to home, the one at my workplace.

"Rose?" Duncan's hand rested lightly on my shoulder, and I blinked, emerging from the shadowy world I'd been inhabiting.

The meeting was getting under way again, and I followed Duncan wordlessly to my chair. The person acting as president had just cleared her throat to speak when the door burst open and a man strode in.

Just past forty, he was tall and only slightly on the stocky side. He worked to keep off the paunch of middle-age, arms and legs still firm and muscled. The worn denim trousers he sported hugged trim thighs. Shirtsleeves were rolled up to reveal admirable biceps. He had that lovely, glossy black hair of the Native American in Karen's portrait, grown just over the top of his collar, and piercing dark eyes that swept the room in greeting and settled instantly on me, the only newcomer.

I shifted in my seat and glanced down at my papers, unsettled by the appraisal, and waited to be introduced. There was no need for anyone to tell me his name, of course. Even if I didn't recognize him from the newspaper photograph, his bearing alone made it clear. This was Peter Moore, leader of the group.

Duncan did the honors. "Pete, this is Rose Claypool,

our new archivist at the school. Remember, I was telling you?"

Pete nodded, an abrupt movement, and stepped across the room, hand outstretched. "Glad you could join us," he told me, his hand engulfing mine in a firm shake. For the space of a heartbeat, our eyes met and again I had that unmistakable feeling of being sized up.

He took his place at the head of the table, and while Karen read the minutes from the first portion of the meeting, he listened intently, nodding approval or making a few notes of his own on the legal pad he'd carried with him.

I could understand his questioning glance at me. A controversial group, conducting itself in a way that challenged the status quo, would always be subject to intrusion by outsiders. For all he knew, I could be a reporter, gathering information on the group's next plan. I could even be from the historical society, which was their target, trying to find out their next scheme. He had only Duncan's word on my identity.

Apparently that was enough.

He showed no hesitation in discussing the latest communiqué from the authorities regarding the return of the artifacts held by the historical society. After twenty minutes of discussion detailing a letter-writing campaign to local newspapers and news releases to other media, Pete asked if there was any new business to discuss.

Duncan sent a sidelong glance at me, and I knew what he was thinking. Would he have a story to tell if the treaty was genuine!

I gave him a wink of conspiracy, and he grinned, looking away. There were a few suggestions for fund-raisers from the members, and the topic was halfheartedly tossed around for a while. Then, consulting a ledger-sized calendar, Pete chose the next meeting date and tonight's gathering was adjourned.

Since Duncan seemed intent on lingering to speak further with Pete, I took a moment to glance into the parking lot once more. Whoever drove that car was definitely putting in some overtime. It still sat in stately silence down below.

Stifling a yawn, I moved to Duncan's side in a less than subtle way to hurry him along. Pete, too, appeared ready to leave and, with Karen joining us, we walked to the elevator.

Pete slipped his arm around Karen's shoulders, and I saw her glance up at him in affection. Karen and Pete? He had to be a good fifteen years older than she was! Love knows no bounds, to be sure, but I was still surprised. It did explain part of Karen's dilemma, however. Pete seemed like a busy man, caught up in his work and his cause.

He could break her heart, I thought as the elevator doors opened.

Standing close to Pete in the tiny cubicle, I was surprised to smell the faint scent of cigarette smoke that clung to his clothing and resisted the urge to wrinkle my nose.

In the parking lot Pete turned to me and stretched out a hand. "I'm glad you came tonight, Rose, and I'm looking forward to working with you."

I clasped his hand briefly and released it. "Thank you," I said. "I'd like to help out." My words were sincere, and Pete smiled, the gesture revealing two rows of broad, gleaming teeth. "Good night." I stepped away, allowing the others to make their farewells.

A few seconds later Duncan caught up with me, falling into step as we crossed the lot. I looked over at him and saw from the corner of my eye the figure of Pete, bent low to unlock the door of the big black car.

Chapter Ten

I paused slightly, my steps faltering. At the door of Duncan's car, I looked again to confirm Pete was indeed by the car in question.

"Rose?" Duncan had unlocked the passenger door and hefted it open, waiting like a gentleman for me to climb in.

By the time he had the old car running, Pete and Karen were on their way, moving past us to the exit. Karen waved and I returned the gesture, seeing her yellow scarf once more at the window.

I thought of explaining the incident to Duncan. It would have been fun to say, "I told you so," but he'd already begun to discuss the evening, and I listened distractedly as he prattled on, rehashing the conversations and thinking out loud all the way home. In no time we'd reached my apartment building. He escorted me to the door, pecked me quickly on the cheek, and added a more personal squeeze.

The memory of that squeeze kept me warm as I waited

a few moments later for the bathtub to fill. Perched on the side, I swished my hand through the water as fragrant bubbles multiplied, perfuming the air in the little room.

It had been an interesting day, followed by an equally interesting evening. I could feel the resulting tension lurking in my shoulders and legs and sank with a grateful sigh into the water's embrace. Tipping my head back against the air pillow I always keep stuck at the end of the tub, I closed my eyes and thought about nothing at all. This is much more difficult than it sounds, and within moments my brain was rerunning scenes from the day.

Duncan. Dear Duncan. *Yes,* I thought, smiling faintly, *he is dear to me. Special to me. Maybe he'll be the most special person of all.*

I felt a tingle at that idea. Not an itch, not a restlessness. Not a question. Just a welcome tingle, which I only hoped he shared. Time would tell, I knew, as it always had in the past, and I rather enjoyed this state of happy anticipation. No need to rush or push or make any demands. We had plenty of time. Our entire future, in fact. I giggled with the delight of a schoolgirl, in love for the very first time. And, truly, I was.

Reluctantly I pushed aside those charming ponderings and changed subjects. The relaxing tub could ease the aching in my body, but it couldn't quiet the anxiety I felt about the mystery of the treaty page and its sudden, odd appearance.

I dropped even lower in the water, letting a wave break over my shoulders.

Funny that Pete's car had been at the school, where the treaty was. Could he have known about it? How? Or had he just been at the college to see Karen? The more logical explanation.

So, who had put that treaty in the archives?

I made a mental note to check with Harriet. Maybe that box of old books had appeared when she was the self-styled custodian of the archives. Who else had access to the collection?

I groaned and reached for the washcloth. It seemed everyone in the Western world had access. If not now, then in the past. Harriet, of course. Emily had been readily admitted by the custodian when she asked. Not that I suspected either woman of tampering with the treaty. They just illustrated the utter lack of security at the school. Someone had gotten into the archives and smoked a cigarette. Someone else nearly got away with the Bible.

Oh, wouldn't life be easy if all the mysterious happenings were the work of one person?

The water had grown tepid as I ruminated, and I gave a shiver, then pulled the plug.

Monday morning came too soon for me.

Duncan and I had gone to a movie together Saturday night and had dinner at the Middle Eastern restaurant on Sunday. We'd both been careful to avoid any speculation about the treaty, the Bible theft, and even the nearly forgotten murder of Samuel Felber. That left us with everything else to talk about, and we took full advantage of the opportunity, sharing stories of childhood and first love.

I told him about some of the places I'd lived and what had been the best part of each. He told me tales of growing up as a policeman's son. As a child, he'd thought guns were cool, he said, until one of his father's friends was hit.

"They didn't seem so terrific after that," he said, grimacing with the remembered pain of his own father's death in the line of duty.

Stretching out a hand to cover his, I suggested, "Tell me about your dad, Duncan. What was he like?"

Duncan's eyes lit up, and he gave me that lopsided smile. The gold shone bright in the green of his eyes as he related anecdote after anecdote, ending with an uproarious one about the family's first and only visit to the opera.

"Mom wanted us to be cultured," he explained. "But it was just too much for Dad. When the soprano started to sing, he started to chuckle. Silently at first. His shoulders were shaking so hard, he bumped me. Well, that set me off, and pretty soon we were all fighting back giggles. Mom was ready to kill us, I think, but on the way home she just said, 'At least you all enjoyed it.' And we did."

"Have you been to the opera since?" I asked and was surprised by the answer.

"All the time. I love it now. And it always makes me think of Dad."

Now, walking down the hallway to the archives, I hummed the only bit of opera I know and wished I knew the words so I could sing it out loud.

The melody died on my lips as I flipped on the lights in the room, and I felt the hairs stand up on the back of my neck.

Something was different. I couldn't tell what. Papers I'd left stacked on my desk were still there, I noticed as my eyes swept the room. Garbage can still full, curtains still drawn. Was it my imagination?

Cautiously I advanced into the room, slowly circling on tiptoe. The silence hung heavily, ringing in my ears, and I found myself straining to hear . . . nothing.

It's an eerie feeling, the one where you sense something out of place, when you feel someone's left a presence in an empty room. My examination of the archives didn't reveal any evidence, but I couldn't shake that crazy sensation. At my desk I did a quick survey of the papers stacked to one side, reaching to my left to gather them up.

And that was the confirmation I'd been hoping for. I'd left the papers piled on the right. The box of stuff for Duncan had been on the other side. Of course, that was gone now, safely stored in Duncan's office.

Well, there wasn't time to dwell on this latest intrusion. I had a lot of work to accomplish before my meeting with Dr. Brossman at eleven o'clock. He'd been reluctant to see me when I called with my request, not deeming my vague explanation very important. I'd had to be aggressively insistent before he relented and promised to squeeze me in. Even then, he'd made it clear he was doing me a favor. My thanks had been profuse, and I'd been angry with myself for allowing him to make me feel intimidated. Now I just wanted to lose myself in my work.

Rolling up my sleeves, I got busy but couldn't resist mentally rehearsing my presentation to the college president. It would be short and focused, and then the situation would be out of my hands.

Around ten o'clock my stomach gave a rumble of

complaint, demanding more than two slices of toast to function. After a few moments' debate, I opted for food. It would only take a short while to nip down to the commons for a hot cup of coffee and a sweet roll. *Ah,* I thought, locking the door of the archives and testing it with a rattle, *the breakfast of champions.*

I stopped in the mailroom to check my box. There'd been no further anonymous notes for me. A small favor, but one I was grateful for. On my way out I nearly bumped into Lily, moving at her usual no-nonsense pace. She had her head down, examining a bunch of notices, and if I hadn't danced two steps to the left, those papers would have flown all over when we collided.

"Lily!" I greeted her with a smile. It was always nice to see her. She never failed to pass along the sort of gossipy information I loved to hear, and I was looking forward to her reaction to news of the treaty. With minimal persuasion she agreed to accompany me, and soon we were sitting at the familiar table near the window, sipping coffee and tucking into a cinnamon-iced sticky bun.

"So what's new?" she asked in all innocence. "How's Duncan?"

I felt my cheeks grow hot as I blushed and said, "Fine, thanks."

"Fine, thanks," she echoed, looking up from her plate, brows knit in disbelief. Laying her knife on the edge of the plate, she licked sweet goop off one finger and demanded, "You'll have to do better than that."

I gave her a brief synopsis of our activities over the weekend—the movies, dinner—and concluded with a gush, "It was wonderful!"

"Well, I must say, I never would have pegged this as the site for budding romance." Her eyes swiveled over our drab surroundings, and I had to agree.

I sipped my coffee, then shrugged. "Stranger things have happened." A pause for dramatic effect. "Truly."

"I'll take that bait. What's up?"

Scooting my chair closer to hers, I took a quick glance to either side. The tables nearest us were empty. Then, dropping my voice to a conspirator's whisper, I leaned on my elbows and spilled the beans.

When I'd told my story, she let out a long whistle that would have made Duncan proud and shot her eyebrows up in shocked surprise. "Oh, a mystery! I love a mystery! You mean, if any descendants are found and if the college is built on that parcel of land, they'd have to knock down the school to reclaim it?"

"Hang on! That's if this document is genuine." I sipped my coffee. "Frankly, I find it highly suspect."

"Oh, well, then there's no mystery." Lily sounded disappointed.

"But then the mystery is—where did it come from?" I reminded her, and her eyes sparked at the changing puzzle.

"Yes!"

We were still ruminating over the matter when Duncan fairly flew into the room. He paused just inside the doorway, skidding to a stop and looking in both directions, surveying the large commons for who knew what.

I did. I stood up and called his name. He looked over, and his eyes lit with recognition. He flapped a hand in greeting, starting over to us without delay.

As we watched him approach, his face set with grim

determination, Lily quipped, "Why am I filled with the irresistible urge to hum 'Taps'?" Then, suiting her words to action, she began the mournful tune.

When he was near enough, Duncan heard her and slid into one of the empty chairs without smiling. "What's that for?" he asked in all seriousness.

"You!" Lily told him. "You've got a face like a storm cloud. How come?"

Duncan looked at me, and I said, "Lily knows about the papers we found."

"And Brossman? What does he say?"

I shrugged. "Nothing yet. He can't see me until eleven. Want to come along?"

He snuck a look at his watch. "It's nearly that now. Sure, I'll come. I'm glad I found you. I've been down-town this morning, to the hall of records."

"Oh?"

"Yes. I needed to dig up a few more tidbits for some of the centennial events, so I thought, as long as I was there, I'd try to trace ownership of Lunham's land. The information needs to be retrieved, though, and they said they'd call as soon as it was available. I did discover that treaty additions like the one in question weren't exactly common practice, but they weren't unknown, either."

"Which means what?" Lily asked the question I wanted to, so I just nodded and urged him on by prodding his foot under the table.

Sternly looking from Lily to me, he said, "Which means we're still in the dark."

"And that isn't all," Lily added sagely, pausing to get our attention before going on. "You're also going to be late if you don't leave right now!"

I gasped, feeling my heart race with agitation over the impending discussion, and pushed back my chair.

Duncan took my hand as we hurried away, and I called over my shoulder, "Wish us luck!"

Lily waved, coffee cup in one hand. "You'll need it."

An hour later we were back in the archives, mission accomplished.

"Well, that wasn't so bad," I confessed, and Duncan shrugged.

"Could have been worse," he agreed.

I sank down onto my desk chair and propped my head up with one hand. "At least he's been informed and the ball is, technically, in his court. He's contacting the attorney, who will contact the experts, who will give us an official verdict, and that's pretty well that."

"I suppose so."

We were interrupted by a tap on the door, which opened to reveal Lily.

"Hope I'm not intruding," she said, closing the door behind her, "but I saw you two go by, and I just had to know what happened. I didn't hear any explosions."

"There weren't any," I told her. "He looked at the treaty, thanked us for telling him, and said he'd get in touch with the college's lawyer right away. He didn't seem overly concerned at all."

"No," Duncan added, "not at all. And he used complete sentences throughout."

"Well! That is surprising." Lily leaned up against a filing cabinet, crossing her arms, and shook her head in disbelief. "Frankly, I expected another scene like the one on the night Sam Felber dared to question his budgeting procedures. He really hit the roof then, remember?" She directed her question to Duncan.

"No," Duncan replied. "I missed that meeting. I sure heard about it, though."

"Yes, didn't we all?" When I looked quizzical, Lily filled me in. "At the same meeting where Brossman's budget was questioned, Sam Felber also brought up closing the weekend program to save money."

I frowned. "And wasn't that the night Felber was killed too?"

Lily nodded, her expression solemn. "It certainly was. And, frankly, just between us, I've always kind of wondered if. . . ." She let the sentence trail off, lifting her shoulders to complete the idea.

I sank into my desk chair, my mouth gaping open as I followed her thought. "You don't really think, not even for a minute. . . ."

Duncan threw up his hands. He regarded us both with a look of unconcealed, utter amazement. "I don't believe you two!" he cried. "Here we are, in the midst of a genuine dilemma, and you start constructing murder plots out of thin air!"

Such a judgmental remark didn't sit well with me, a fact I thought Duncan would have realized long ago. Drawing myself up, I retorted, "Hardly from thin air, Duncan. A body was found, you'll recall."

"That's right!" Lily joined in. "Somebody killed him, and Brossman is as good a guess as any."

"Fine. Go ahead and waste your time on ridiculous speculation. Maybe you can even decide who killed JFK." He glanced at his wristwatch and delivered a parting shot neither of us could argue with. "I've got a class to teach." The door didn't exactly slam behind him, but it did close with a resounding thump.

"Oh, honestly!" Lily grimaced at the noise, then shook her head in dismissal. "So, what about Brossman?"

Half an hour later our well had run dry, and Lily rose from her place on the corner of the desk.

"I guess I should get back. If anyone decides she needs career counseling and I'm not around, Brossman is sure to hear of it."

"Before you go, though, could you help me with an errand?" I asked, already gathering up an artist's palette and several dried brushes from where Karen had left them the last time she'd worked on the mural. "These were left behind, and I've been meaning to return them to the art department."

"What is it with you and paint?" Lily teased as we set off down the hall. "I'm getting this odd sense of déjà vu."

"Oh, very funny."

A class was in progress when we poked our heads around the door, and Emily greeted us with a questioning smile. A dozen students looked our way, interrupting their work momentarily.

"Um." I held up the paints and Lily waved the brushes.

"On the back counter, please," Emily directed and returned to her lecture.

Walking on tiptoe, we crossed the room, clearing a space on the crowded surface to deposit our burden.

As I turned away, I saw once more the elaborate red banner celebrating the school's centennial. It looked complete now, every available space covered with design and sequins or baubles. The enticing color drew my eye, and I couldn't resist reaching out to trace the delicate outline of a floral appliqué.

"Beautiful," I said quietly, but not quietly enough.

Emily broke off to tell me, "Tomorrow it will be hung in the main stairwell, Rose. Be sure you stop to take a look at it there."

Picturing the artwork so brilliantly displayed, I bobbed my head. "Count on it!"

The next morning sunshine heralded almost spring-like weather, although in October I knew it was only nature's jest. Still, I was more than happy to don well-worn sneakers with my work clothes, carrying my pumps in a plastic sack, and walk the short distance from my apartment to the college.

When I turned the corner onto the long tree-lined avenue that always reminded me of the approach to Windsor Castle, my eye immediately picked out the creamy brick box that was the ad-lib building. For one hundred years it had looked like this, nestled snugly in the trees at the end of the road. In fact, the very next evening would mark the beginning of the centennial events. Duncan's lecture on the history of the state was designed as a prelude to the big event—the unveiling of Emily's banner in the stairwell and the mural in the archives.

I'd spend my day tidying up, which would probably consist of shoving everything possible into my little storage room and slamming the door. No one would be examining my work quite yet, so all I needed for the evening was a semblance of order, and that's probably all I'd manage.

After the bright light of the morning, I blinked as I entered the dim building, moving slowly until my eyes adjusted. I stopped at my mailbox and was relieved to see the usual round of humdrum meeting notices and a student newsletter. At least there was no mystery mail today. Whoever sent the first one must have realized I was here to stay. The thought made me smile as I headed for the archives. I was still thinking when I came up the stairwell closest to the archives door and fished for my key.

I reached the door, key extended, just as Harriet, the librarian, opened it and emerged from inside. She looked furtive and startled at my sudden appearance, an expression I'm sure I returned.

Frowning, I wondered what business she had within the locked confines of the archives. I took a step toward her. She had a manila folder tucked under one arm, her elbow firmly in place to prevent it from slipping.

"Good morning, Harriet," I greeted her civilly enough. "May I ask what you were doing in there?" I jerked my head to indicate the archives.

She reached up to nervously tweak an overpermed lock of gray hair. This morning she was done up in brown—cabled cardigan, plaid skirt, sensible shoes. When she answered, her voice was loud with unjustified defiance.

"I needed to check a reference, that's all. About . . . um, about the previous presidents of the college. I didn't disturb anything, so you don't have to worry."

"Oh, I'm not worried," I assured her, making my words casual, to suit my attitude. I approached the door, opening it when she stepped aside. "Please, come in and I'll help you find that material."

Harriet stalled for time. She hadn't been looking for anything particular, I knew in a flash. She'd merely been snooping. Realizing it looked odd to neither accept nor decline my invitation, she looked longingly down the hall toward escape.

"Harriet?" I prodded, pushing my advantage.

"Oh, all right," she snapped and came inside. "I've already turned up what I need, though, actually. And . . . and I must say you're working wonders in here." The false praise was betrayed by her darting eyes.

I took a moment to hang up my coat on a hook in the tiny storage room, then advanced on the filing cabinet where the clippings and bios of former presidents were located. Pulling out an overlong manila folder, I extended it with a bit of flourish.

"Lucky you finding it, when I haven't had time to relabel these drawers. Did you just rummage around looking?"

She flushed, taking the folder from me and looking down into its contents. "Your tone isn't very pleasant, Rose. I almost feel as if you are accusing me of something."

I took my seat at the little desk and shrugged. Picking up a handful of unsorted correspondence I'd tossed there yesterday, I made mention of my concerns about security, my knowledge of intruders in the archives.

"Oh, I suppose you think I did it, just because I was in here this morning!" she exclaimed, slapping the folder down on the top of a cabinet.

"Did I say that?" I challenged without looking up. A suspicious envelope in the stack of papers on my desk had caught my eye. I lifted it out of the pile with cautious fingers, as if it could bite me.

Over my shoulder I heard Harriet draw in a tight breath. I could feel her watching me as I slit the seal and drew out a sheet of typing paper.

" 'Curiosity killed the cat,' " I read aloud, leaning back in my chair with the paper held at arm's length. "What do you suppose that means?" I spun my chair around, facing Harriet and flapping the paper at her. "Any ideas?"

Her mouth gaped open and closed again, and she blinked rapidly behind the thick lenses of her glasses. "I . . . I. . . ."

"Yesterday this envelope wasn't here. This morning it is. And so are you. If I dusted this for prints, Harriet, would they turn out to be yours?"

For an instant I thought she'd deny my charge and storm out. Instead of exploding, however, she imploded. Her eyes widened, and, magnified as they were, they looked ready to pop from their sockets. Hands clenched into fists at her sides, she sent me a malevolent glare that gave me a chill. Her words were more startling than her rage, however, when she delivered them in barely controlled fury.

"Ever since you came here, you've been nothing but trouble," she accused me. "Taking this job away from me when I was doing a perfectly adequate job. Wasting money we could have used for other, truly important things. I don't know what that alumna was thinking of, making us hire you when so many issues are more pressing."

She moved closer, leaning over me to lecture directly into my face. "And don't think I haven't heard about the questions you've been asking—about that murder, about the school charter."

"Charter? You mean the treaty?" I clarified, sitting up straighter.

She waved a hand dangerously close to my nose. "Whatever it was! It's all over the school, you know. If that thing is real, we'll probably all lose our jobs. Unemployed! We'll be unemployed and on the street because you had to be so thorough and nosy!"

One of my questions had just been answered. She obviously had never seen the treaty, hidden away in that book. Now knowledge of it had her terrified, and the force of that terror was directed at me.

I frowned. My heart was pounding with a combination of anger and fear. I didn't have to stretch very far to see that dear Harriet was at least one bubble off plumb, and part of me wondered if she actually planned to do me physical harm. I had no idea how to defuse her. My education wasn't in psychology, after all. I took the defensive, which was probably the wrong thing to do.

"How do you know about the treaty page?" I asked. "Who told you?" A futile question. The small-town grapevine that existed at the school would pass any news like a brushfire.

Harriet smirked unbecomingly. "Wouldn't you like to know?" she teased in a childish fashion, stopping just short of sticking out her tongue. "I have friends around here. Real friends. And they tell me plenty, miss."

"And are they part of your campaign to drive me out?" I demanded, standing up and forcing her to take a step back. "Or do you always act alone? Leaving silly notes, calling me and hanging up. Moving things around so I can't find them. What do you think Dr. Brossman will say when I tell him? Or is he one of your friends?" I challenged. I wasn't positive she was responsible for the phone calls and the rearranged articles, but it seemed a good bet, since she'd all but confessed to the mystery notes.

She took a moment to look frightened, realizing she'd overstepped her boundaries. Plucking at the button on her cardigan, she visibly deflated. "Oh, you mustn't tell. No, no. Never tell. Just a bit of mischief. That's all it was. No harm done. Surely you can see that," she babbled in a rush. "If you just mind your own business, it won't ever happen again," she promised, reluctant to concede the argument without scoring some points.

I shook my head. "No deals, Harriet. I want you to leave me alone. I'm doing the job I was hired to do, and I don't need any input from you. All this can remain just between the two of us, but if I get one more note or phone call or if one more paper is moved as much as an inch, I'm going directly to the president! Do we understand each other?"

I'd wagged my finger at her as I spoke, and she'd backed up a few paces, holding her folder full of papers defensively in front of her body. Now she swallowed convulsively, knowing I meant business. She took a step to the left, determined to go around me and escape without answering.

I, too, moved left, into her path and she groaned in frustration. "All right! All right! You have my promise. Now, let me pass!"

She pushed by me, catching the edge of her folder against my elbow. It slipped, tipping from beneath her arm. We both made a grab to catch it, but our attempts failed, and the folder dropped to the floor, spilling its contents across the tiles.

Several papers, a few photographs, and a stack of note cards scattered in a fan, and on top of it all lay a faded pink ribbon adorned with gemstones glittering under the lights.

I didn't believe my eyes then, and I still didn't believe it later. Not even hours later, after Harriet had babbled and reasoned and pleaded.

I'd snatched up the ribbon and run for the phone, telling Dr. Brossman to come at once, the jewels were back. He could get the rest of the picture on arrival.

Harriet had seemed too stunned to move at first, looking crumpled and faded. When Dr. Brossman came puffing into the archives, she'd blinked, coming out of her trance, then began to jabber out a series of lies by way of explanation.

"Oh, Dr. Brossman, thank goodness you're here!" she cried, rushing over and clasping his hand. "Just look what I found in the archives, sir. Hidden away in a drawer where she hoped no one would find it." Harriet tugged the president over to my desk, where I stood sentinel over the precious bookmark.

Dr. Brossman looked from Harriet to the bookmark to me. I opened my mouth to begin my defense, but Harriet cut me off.

"I suspected it from the start, sir. First she comes here, then trouble starts. I knew she was the thief! You'd better call the police. I'm sure they'll want to arrest her."

Brossman patted Harriet's hand where it still rested on his arm, then disengaged himself. "What do you have to say, Ms. Claypool? How did this marker get here?"

I answered him truthfully. "All I can tell you is it fell out of Harriet's folder. She was in the archives before I arrived this morning, and I think she meant to plant the bookmark here, so you would think I had stolen it."

Clenching her hands into fists, Harriet shook her head and raged, "That is not true! I planned no such thing. I . . . I . . . I came for some information, that's all!"

I pushed on. "I think she heard me coming and tried to sneak out before I surprised her. She didn't have time to plant the bookmark, but she did leave me this love note."

He took the envelope I offered and read the message within. Giving a sigh, he turned to Harriet and spoke calmly. "All right, let's hear the truth now, dear. Would you like to tell me?"

"You'd believe her over me?" One pointy finger jabbed at me.

"Yes, I would," Dr. Brossman said. "Because I know about your little anonymous notes. Remember, I spoke to you about this before, when you were threatening that student with all the overdues."

Harriet colored, her cheeks turning ruddy in uneven patches. "But that girl had several volumes of a very important reference tool," she said. "And I did get them back!"

"After leaving the student notes like this." The paper flapped in Brossman's hand. Physical evidence.

Harriet pressed her lips together and looked down without saying a word.

"Come on, Harriet. There won't be any trouble. Just tell me the truth," Brossman urged while I stood by in silence.

With a sigh of resignation, Harriet agreed in a dull voice, "Oh, very well. I just did it for the college, you know."

What it boiled down to, we realized after a lengthy discussion, was that Harriet had truly been the thief.

"We don't need a ten-thousand dollar bookmark," Harriet sneered. "A grand gesture but a useless one. We need cash, Dr. Brossman, as you well know. Lunham's in big trouble, and I thought, well. . . ." She looked at her clasped hands, twisting them together and collecting a deep breath before going on.

Over her head Dr. Brossman and I exchanged a look of caution, waiting.

"If the ribbon was stolen, we could collect the insurance money. The bookmark was safe with me, so Lunham could have its cake and eat it too. It's so simple." A tender smile touched the corner of her mouth. "You do see?"

Dr. Brossman cleared his throat. "I see you meant well. But you did the wrong thing. You shouldn't have stolen the marker, and you'll have to give it back." He spoke gently, quietly, surprising me by his grasp of the delicate situation.

"But the money!" Harriet exclaimed.

Placing a heavy hand on her shoulder, he said, "We've been in tough spots before and managed to survive, dear. We always land on our feet."

To me, he went on. "I'll explain the matter to the authorities and tell them the college won't be pressing charges. Then I'll arrange for some counseling for Harriet."

I nodded, finding the diplomatic solution to be the best one possible. *Poor Dr. Brossman,* I thought as he led Harriet away. *This has been a rough week, and it's not over yet!*

Chapter Eleven

The night of Duncan's lecture, the meeting room filled quickly with about fifty people from the staff, student body, community, and media. The din of many separate conversations echoed across the space, punctuated by laughter here and there. Someone close by had had a heavy hand with the after-shave, and I wrinkled my nose as I surveyed the people around me.

When I'd talked with Duncan earlier, he'd been composed and prepared for the presentation. Watching him stride confidently to the podium, I felt a burst of pride in him and smiled warmly, hoping he could find me in the sea of faces.

The crowd settled down as he greeted us; then he launched into a lively and fascinating portrayal of the state's history. In his hands the potentially dry information came to life, peopled with living human beings whose struggles and triumphs had shaped the world we lived in.

I glanced around the room, watching people respond to Duncan's monologue, and spotted plenty of familiar faces. Georgia Spencer, Emily, Lily. Karen was seated next to Pete, her eyes on Duncan, but Pete was carrying on an intense conversation with the man on his right. The dark-haired man had his head tipped to catch Pete's words and was tugging at his tie in an automatic gesture. Several times he nodded in response and added a few words of his own.

I frowned, wondering what they were discussing. I knew Duncan had not mentioned the treaty to anyone, and yet, since the document was uppermost in my mind, my first instinct told me it was their topic. Of course, as Harriet had been so quick to inform me, the news was all over the school now, so it was quite possible the outside world had also heard.

I tuned back into Duncan's lecture, and soon all thoughts of mystery slipped away. The lights were dimmed for a slide presentation, and I recognized several photos as ones I had provided from the archives. Through the pictures we saw the fashions change, horse-drawn carriages replaced by automobiles and streetcars, and, finally, freeways. Small hamlets became big cities, and skyscrapers began to appear. Our journey through the past continued, bringing us up to the present day with a closing slide of the college, surrounded by the beautiful trees of autumn, looking for all the world like a marvelously executed painting.

Rousing applause greeted Duncan as he concluded, "And now we'll all get a chance to view the latest treasures here at Lunham College. Please follow me to the north stairwell, where Emily Welbourne's stunning centennial banner is on display. Then we'll move to the archives and view the new mural illustrating the founding of the college. This work was completed by Ms. Welbourne and her students, and I'm sure you'll find it delightful."

Everyone stood up at once, and suddenly fifty people were scrambling to be first out the door. I shuffled along with the crowd, inching toward the door, where Duncan stood.

When I got within a few feet of him, he shot out a hand and clasped my elbow, pulling me out of line. "Rose! I need your help!" he pleaded, still smiling and nodding at the people moving past us.

"Why? What's up?"

"Well, it's the reception. After the tour there's a wine-and-cheese reception upstairs, you know? And I wanted to display a few historical articles around the tables. Visual appeal."

"Yes, yes. What's the problem?"

He sighed and ran a hand through his hair. "Remember that daguerreotype of old man Lunham as a child? The one that showed four generations of the family?"

I shut my eyes, trying to recall the picture. I'd seen so many in recent weeks, it was difficult to keep them straight. At last I said, "The one with the little old lady who looked like a shrunken apple doll?"

"That's right. Ella Lunham. Do you think you could find it? I'd like to place it near the centerpiece. There's already an old newspaper, the first college catalog, and a student photo display, but that family shot would be great, don't you think?"

I grimaced. "Well, Duncan, it sounds like you've already got plenty of stuff. I really don't think you need—"

"Yes, but it would be so perfect! And, really, it would be the only representation of the Lunham family as a family!" He spread his hands for emphasis. "Please," he begged, reaching for my hand and giving it a squeeze.

Who could refuse? Not me. "All right," I said, sighing just a little. "I wish you weren't so persnickety. Do you have any idea where that picture is?"

"No," he said. "Where?"

"That's just it, I'm not sure myself! I bundled up all the jumble and packed it away so the archives would look tidy for tonight! It's somewhere in that little storage room."

"Oh, you'll find it," he assured me. "I know you will. Could you go look right now?"

I gritted my teeth and nodded. Moving away, I told him, "You owe me one, pal."

In the relatively short time I'd been at the college, I'd managed to learn my way around its many complex, honeycombed corridors and stairwells. Moving rapidly, I made it to the archives in about three minutes, puffing only slightly from the exertion.

The corridor around me was silent and empty as I let myself in. Everyone was still in the stairwell, examining the banner.

I snapped on the overhead lights and looked around. The place looked nice, quite neat and tidy, the perfect backdrop for Emily's wonderful mural. I regarded it briefly now as I headed for the storage room.

I had to use my shoulder to push the door open, shoving a box on the other side out of my way.

"Oh!" I groaned as the light in the little room snapped on. This place was the antithesis of the outer archives. Box piled on box in a teetering tower, and all available floor space was covered as well. Through this, I would wade, looking for one little photograph.

"May as well get at it!" I muttered, lifting the lid off one cardboard carton.

As I sifted quickly through each container, I set it aside, building a second tower. Just as I was beginning to despair, I heard voices approaching from the corridor and knew it was time for my stop on the tour. Straightening up, I pressed a hand against my back and wondered how my makeup had fared during this unscheduled exercise.

I kicked aside a carton lid and emerged into the archives just in time to meet the visitors. The oohing and aahing went on for a good twenty minutes as everyone took a close look at the painting.

Emily introduced Karen as one of the student artists, waving her forward to take a bow. I looked to Pete, expecting him to beam in admiration, or at least be paying attention, but he was wandering down one of the aisles, reading the labels on cabinet drawers. The man I'd seen him with earlier stood on the fringe of the crowd, hands in the pockets of his expensive suit coat, rocking back and forth on his heels.

Duncan rushed up, blocking my view, and asked urgently, "Have you found it?"

I hated to tell him. "No, I haven't, but I'll keep looking after everyone leaves."

Duncan shrugged. "Oh, that's okay. Forget it. It doesn't matter," he said in an unconvincing tone.

By now it had become a matter of honor. "I'll find it. I just have a few more boxes to check, but I'll find it."

He gave a big smile, and my heart jumped a bit. "Thanks, Rose. You're the best."

"Well, that's good to know," I teased. "Now, move these folks along so I can get back to the hunt."

He took me at my word, urging everyone along to the reception. As the people began to leave the archives in twos and threes, I slipped back into the storage room and resumed my search.

The next box I opened revealed the oversized book where the treaty had been hidden, and I lifted it out, wishing it could tell me all its secrets. Running a hand across its cover, I wondered how the treaty had ever come to be stored inside it. And what would the experts say? True or false? Genuine or forgery?

I lifted the book cover, and it flopped open, no longer attached to the body of the book. The heady smell of mold and decay wafted out at me. Riffling a few of the weak, yellowed pages, I came to the one displaying the book's title and found scrawled there the owner's name.

Samuel Felber.

It took me a moment to place him. I'd never met him and hadn't been thinking about him on this night. Until now. Samuel Felber. The murdered board member.

I sat back on my heels, pressing my lips together and clutching the book. Odd that the board member who had been killed had owned the book containing this questionable copy of the treaty. More than a coincidence, it would seem. More like a motive.

I blew out a long, full breath and shook my head to clear out the buzzing and rushing in my ears. Why hadn't I noticed this earlier? How had I overlooked such a fascinating and potentially valuable clue?

Was the board member responsible for the forgery? If the treaty were a fake, what possible reason could Sam Felber have for possessing it? It could only harm the school, after all, and surely no board member would want that!

If the treaty were genuine, he'd have a good excuse for suppressing it—protecting the school. And, my imagination raced on, if the legal heirs knew about the treaty and what they stood to gain, they might literally kill for it.

I bit my lip and chewed thoughtfully. It seemed this puzzle had no solution, only more pieces turning up all the time.

Reluctantly I set the book aside, onto the stack of boxes now blocking my way to the door. There'd be time later, after tonight's festivities, to sit down with paper and pencil to ponder the mystery.

I dropped to my knees behind another box to resume work. Beyond, in the outer area, the drone of voices had faded away. I pictured everyone sipping fine wine and nibbling cheese while I burrowed, molelike, through decades of Lunham College history, and I was tempted to give up. But there were only three more boxes to look in, after all, and I pride myself on being very thorough.

Moments later my search was rewarded, and I held in my hand the Lunham family portrait. Sitting back on my heels, I sighed in relief. Naturally, the picture had been in the very last box, mixed in with a stack of other old snapshots. Now I had only to move the tower I'd built and clear a path to the door.

Duncan, Duncan, I thought, surveying the jumbled room, *the things I do!* My exasperation was a fond one, though.

It was while I crouched, silently, that I heard a noise in the outer room. The scrape of a shoe against the floor tile was followed by the low murmur of voices. Someone had lingered for a lengthy examination of the mural, I guessed, but I didn't make a sound as I pressed my hand against the cool floor and rose. Tucking the old picture inside Sam Felber's book, I slipped the book under my arm and stepped silently around the mountain of boxes into an open space just behind the door.

I could recognize the voices now as those of two men having a heated discussion. As I got close to the door of the storage room, I was able to make out their conversation.

"Pete, do you mind telling me what we're doing here?" The man's voice held more than a little impatience.

Clutching the old book tightly to my chest, I took a step forward, putting my eye just above the hinge on the door. The crack was only about a half-inch wide, but it afforded me a partial view of the room. The man who had spoken was the same well-varnished person Pete had been conversing with during Duncan's lecture. He paced a few steps, paused to sniff the air, then joked, "Nice perfume, buddy. Chanel?"

I stiffened in my hiding place. He could smell my fragrance. Would he investigate? I had no desire to be discovered eavesdropping, but I needn't have worried.

"Ah, that's Rose. She smells good. Looks good too." Pete dismissed the detail. His next words were loud and clear as he said in agitation, "That book has to be here somewhere, Alex! I didn't hide it that well!"

Book? Hidden?

The treaty! My mind supplied the answer quickly and without hesitation.

Pete was sitting at my desk, legs crossed, one foot jogging nervously. His fingers drummed a staccato rhythm on the tabletop. Again he spoke, his voice displaying the same anxiety. "I tell you, I put that old book in a box with a bunch of others and set the whole thing down next to a stack of newspapers and file folders. Now, where is it?"

The man named Alex strode into view, one hand jangling the change in his pocket. "I guess you didn't put it in plain view. Maybe this lady isn't very smart and she missed it."

"Missed it? How could she miss it? It was right under her nose!" Pete snapped, leaning forward and gesturing angrily.

Alex shrugged. His expensive shoes clicked heavily against the floor tiles as he took another turn around the room. "Then how come we haven't heard anything about the treaty? You're sure this Duncan would come straight to you?"

I sucked in a breath, my heart sinking painfully. Duncan? Involved in something nefarious? *No,* my heart told me. *Never!*

Pete smirked, his lips twisting into a grimace of disgust. "Oh, yeah. I'm sure. The minute Duncan gets wind of that treaty page, he'll come running. 'Look-ee, look-ee! See what I found!' " He mimicked an eager child, clamoring for approval. "Then I read it, look startled, and say 'Why, my great-great-great-great granddad was Chief White Star! And that must mean—' "

"Yes, yes," Alex cut into Pete's performance. "You're the heir, the land is yours. I know how the action was supposed to go, Pete. But it hasn't exactly worked out that way." Parking one hip on the corner of my desk, his hands dangled in studied nonchalance. "Perhaps you underestimated Duncan, picked the wrong pawn."

My legs were cramping, tensed as they were, and the book in my arm grew heavier and more cumbersome with each minute. I didn't dare risk moving, however. The slightest sound from me, and they'd be wrenching open the door to reveal me, crouched and cowering like a mouse in a trap.

It was clear to me now that Pete had planned to use Duncan for his scheme, whatever it was. Use us both, actually, knowing I would confide my discovery in Duncan immediately.

"Wrong pawn?" Pete repeated. "No way! He was perfect. Totally innocent, getting the news from another innocent source."

"You're sure this Rose would let him in on the news?" Alex asked.

"Oh, yeah!" Pete assured him. "Karen told me those two are thick. Quite an item here at school." He nodded. "She'd tell him, all right."

My cheeks burned in anger at being so easily dismissed. *Poor Karen,* I thought. *She must not know about this. She's been taken in too.*

Alex shook his head, not a hair moving out of place. "I don't know, Pete. Maybe we ought to just give it up. This is turning into more than I bargained for."

"What?" Pete jumped to his feet, startling me with the quick action.

I took a step back involuntarily, bumping a carton lid. The noise it made as it skidded a few inches was loud in my ears, but the men in the room just beyond never seemed to notice. Gingerly I applied my eye to the crack again.

"Some lawyer you are! Where are your teeth? Your guts? We're not stopping now! Look, I'll be the first to admit maybe I didn't do a picture-perfect job—" Pete broke off as Alex interrupted with a great snort of laughter. "But," he continued, "it's all going according to plan."

"Well, now, be honest, Pete. Murder was never part of the plan."

My hand shot up to cover my mouth, hiding my gasp of shock. I pressed my eye closer to the crack, leaning against the wall of the tiny room as my legs quaked beneath me. The words had come out of left field, totally unexpected, and as my brain shifted and sorted, I missed Pete's curse of agreement. When I tuned back in, he was still speaking.

"I should have known Sam would turn out to be a greedy old bugger. It was a mistake to get involved with him, but I needed his connection."

"I must say," Alex admitted, "that treaty page certainly looks authentic. I think it will hold up under examination. It's safe to assume the artist was well paid?" Alex casually dropped another bombshell, and it hit even nearer home this time.

Reaching into the pocket of his coat, Pete withdrew a package of cigarettes and lit one before answering. "Yeah, he was paid." He blew a jet of gray smoke upward. "And I don't think I'll hear from him again. Sam was the only one changing the rules as he went along."

"Foolish old man," Alex agreed with a hint of something like regret in his voice. The show of emotion seemed foreign and anything but genuine.

"It would have been a sweet deal for him," Pete put in. "Provide the forgery and share in the millions when we sold the land to the developers." He shook his head.

"Biggest mall in the state, Pete. Cripes, it'll be a city in itself! Now Lunham Ridge will be built, and he'll never see a cent of the profit."

Developers! Mall! The flash of understanding that hit me came as a blinding-white light. I closed my eyes against it, and the plan became clear.

The three men—Pete, Alex, and Sam—had created a scheme to get their hands on the land owned by Lunham College. The forged treaty page, if it held up in court, would turn the acreage over to Pete Moore. Pete would then sell it to a developer as a site for a shopping mall! I remembered reading about a proposed mall drawing protest in a city nearby. Pete must have thought to sway the developers into building here instead. Until Sam complicated things. Probably wanting more money.

I could almost picture the scene. Pete and Sam, together at a rendezvous after that agitated board meeting. Sam laying his demands on the table. Pete disagreeing, arguing. Shouting. Shoving. Picking up a rock or a tree branch and bringing it down with fatal force.

I shuddered at the violence from the past and the ever-present potential for more. A chill crept up my backbone, spreading throughout each limb until my teeth were ready to chatter. I kept my jaw slack to prevent it and sent up prayers for a safe way out of this horrible, horrible spot.

When I was a child and in a bad situation—picked on by some bigger kids, first day in another new school, in trouble with Mom or Dad—I'd picture a peaceful scene, with me right in the middle of it. I tried now to see a meadow or a waterfall, but all I could see was the woods behind the college and a body crumpled there.

Oh, Duncan, I thought, tears of fear prickling my eyes and burning the back of my throat, *help me, please!* And then, *No, no! Don't come! Don't come looking for me! Don't let them see you and wonder where I am!* I had to swallow hard and focus on something familiar, the sight of the telephone, to keep my wits clear. My eyes studied the simple black object as these two ruthless men continued their tea party.

"So, how did you hit on this book idea, anyway?" Alex asked. He'd wandered out into the aisles now, and I couldn't see him any longer. He was opening and closing cabinet drawers, and I heard the rustle of paper in my files.

Pete was happy to explain. "Sam had it in his car the night I . . . he. . . . Well, that night. I lifted it. Wasn't any use to him anymore. Then I planted it here." His words were bald and unadorned.

Alex's voice held a hint of admiration. "Good work. Very logical. Worthy of me. Now, if only we can find the darn thing!" They both chuckled at that, partners in crime and proud of it.

In my hiding place I sneered in revulsion. If I weren't witnessing the event with my own eyes and ears, I'd never have believed it. Pete Moore, crusading Native American, leading his group and earning their trust. Were any of his emotions genuine? I wondered. Did he have any sense of commitment to the cause he so publicly espoused, or was it all part of this sham? I recalled the protest at the historical society and Pete's speech. When I'd read it in the newspaper, I'd agreed with the man and the excellent remarks he'd made.

A new wave of anger washed over me, at the damage this selfish man had done to his group and their sincere efforts. He'd taken their trust and used it for his own purpose and, public opinion being a fickle creature, there would be serious repercussions for the group. Allegations to deny, respect to win back. Pete Moore's crimes went way beyond murder and fraud, jeopardizing the local Native American movement. He'd acted as a con man, and if I had anything to say about it, soon the world would know.

A metal drawer clanged shut, and Alex gave a moan. "This is insane. We'll never find that thing tonight. For all we know, it's not even in this room. What's in there?"

I didn't need to guess where he was pointing. Shrinking back against the wall and dropping down low, I tried to flatten myself out. The book in question burned my hands, and my knees shook with fear. If they found me now, I was good as dead.

The desk chair was pushed back, giving a screech against the tiles, and I heard Pete groan to his feet. Crossing the space quickly, he put a hand to the storage-room door and pushed.

I shut my eyes, making myself invisible, I hoped.

The door smacked into my displaced tower of cartons and stopped, having moved only six inches. I held my breath as Pete poked his nose around the corner.

"Man, what a mess!" he said, and I had to agree. "If this is all she's managed to accomplish, old Lunham isn't getting its money's worth," he added with a chuckle.

In my cramped position, I grimaced. Oh, he was so funny. I tipped my head to one side, peeking out above the hinge near the floor.

Flicking the storage room light off, Pete turned on his heel and walked back to the desk, tapping his fingers against the blotter.

I blinked at the sudden darkness but made no move. My tower of boxes became square black mountains, silhouetted by the meager light coming in from the outer room.

"Look—" Alex held up a hand as a brainstorm hit. "You told me you've got a key to this place, right?"

Holding in a groan, I thought, *Another key!*

"Yes—"

"Well, let's come back some night this week and look again. Maybe she'll find the treaty by then. Or have the place cleaned up so we can. If we stay here much longer, someone is sure to wonder what we're up to."

Pete nodded. "I suppose. I just want to get this show on the road, and all these delays are making me angry." His fist came down hard and suddenly, banging the desk and making the pencil cup jump.

"Just be glad you've got the key so we have an option," Alex told him. He paused for thought. "Do I want to know how you got that key?"

Pete shrugged. "I picked it up one day when I came here to see Karen. Stopped at the information booth for directions. No one was around, but there was a map of the campus on the wall behind the desk. And right next to the phone was a piece of pegboard filled with neatly labeled keys. I couldn't believe it!" he laughed.

I could. I'd seen that pegboard myself. If you stayed on the outside of the booth, you'd never know it was there, tucked under the counter.

"I thought I might need it, so I put it in my pocket." He lifted his shoulders, dismissing the theft.

"You worry me, Pete. You really do," Alex said.

"Well, thanks for the concern, pal," Pete said, "but why don't you save it for another time, huh? Let's get out of here." He took a step toward the door, adding over his shoulder, "I'm just in the mood for a little wine and cheese."

Alex laughed heartily at Pete's adopted snobbish tone and followed him from the room, making a few jokes of his own. They snapped off the light at the door, and the room filled with inky darkness and a heavy silence.

Chapter Twelve

I counted to ten, quickly, and pushed open the storage-room door with a cautious hand. Stepping into the archives, I sprinted for the door. It was dark, and I didn't know the room as well as I imagined. I collided heavily with the corner of a file cabinet and winced in pain, bending over my bruised hip. The last few steps to the corridor, I limped.

At the door to the hall, I paused, listening. No footsteps or voices penetrated the wood. Holding my breath, I eased the door open. I don't know what I expected to see when I glanced out, but there was just the empty hallway, stretching off to the vanishing point.

After closing the archives door behind me, I gave it a push to make sure the lock had caught, then nearly laughed out loud. All the people who had come and gone had used their own keys, and I was making sure the door was locked!

Holding the heavy book across my chest, I moved quickly in the direction of the stairwell, making a mental note to see the custodian about a new lock first thing in the morning. He'd better make it a dead bolt.

As my heels clicked along on the tiles, my brain was struggling to formulate a plan. My breath came in quick, short gasps, and the book thumped clumsily against my body. So far my plan consisted of two steps. Get Duncan. Go to the police. I couldn't imagine confronting the two criminals with public accusations, and the very thought of telling Dr. Brossman made me shudder. Oh, he'd be irate to hear it secondhand from the authorities one more time, but he'd never believe the story if it came directly from me.

Pulling open the door to the stairwell, I pictured the route ahead. Up one flight, down the hall, then right to the meeting room.

The stairs were lit in the same murky fashion as the hall, but it was clear enough for me to see Emily's huge red banner hung on the landing. I took a few valuable seconds to admire the piece, remembering my promise to see it in its prominent position. It stretched the length of two flights of stairs and was nearly as wide—a good six feet across. In the daylight it would be stunning. Now its deep color seemed to swallow the light.

Stretching out a hand, I grasped the metal banister. Above me, the stairs climbed out of sight, spiraling upward. I clambered up a half-dozen steps before I detected motion from above. The sound of my own footsteps had covered other noises, and when I glanced up from my intent concentration on the stairs, my heart gave a frantic leap.

Halfway down the flight above and heading in my direction were Alex and Pete!

We all stopped dead, exchanging looks that charged the air and told it all. I'm no poker face and knew my knowledge of their actions was written in my expression. And if they had any doubts, the cumbersome book I carried would provide all the evidence they'd need.

It was Alex who spoke first, looking down at me from his vantage point. "See," he said to Pete. "I knew that perfume smell was too strong to be from earlier in the day. We had an eavesdropper. What should we do about her?" He moved down a step without ever taking his eyes from my face.

I'd never been in such a terrifying position. All my limbs were quivering with tension as my nerves leaped in hysteria. For several awful seconds I didn't know what to do. I felt a sob rising into a lump in my throat and swallowed hard.

When I looked at Pete, I had a moment's hope. His eyes looked tired, and his lips were drawn down with weariness. He didn't look like a man eager to fight. My brain flashed me a scenario where Pete admitted defeat and came quietly along to the police.

Then he addressed his attorney, and my bubble popped, as they always do. "This project just got a little bloodier, I guess." Each word fell like ice, cold and brittle, and I realized he was calculating my death. Pete had already taken one life to make his scheme reality. Apparently a lowly archivist could also be sacrificed.

Before either man could move another inch, I took a deep breath and opened my mouth. The shriek was high-pitched and as loud as I could muster. It reverberated in the cavernlike area of the stairwell, but even as its first notes were echoing around me, I was turning and charging off back down the steps.

My feet pounded each stair with increasing force, and I kept a firm grasp on the banister. I didn't intend to be like an actress in one of those corny monster films, turning an ankle or breaking a heel at the crucial moment.

I rushed on past the door to the hallway. That floor was deserted. No one could help me there. The next level down contained a student lounge and some study areas. Surely someone would be around. Someone who could call the cops and save my life.

But I never got that far.

When I'd begun my sprint, Alex and Pete had started off in pursuit. I could hear the racket they made chasing after me, cursing at me and at each other. I had a few seconds' head start, but they had longer legs. At one point I risked a glance over my shoulder and saw Pete taking the steps two at a time. He'd reach me in just an instant, I knew, and felt just as the fox must when the hounds come to call.

I propelled myself down the stairs, scrambling pell-mell and continuing the deafening screams. Not unexpected, but nonetheless frightening, Pete's hand grasped my shoulder as he closed in, and I wrenched away. The next time we connected, he was a bit more forceful. Both palms caught me square in the back and sent me reeling off balance. I missed a few steps, hit the landing on one foot, and staggered smack into the wall, struggling to keep from falling.

I put up my hands to ease the impact, finally dropping the big book I'd been compulsively holding. I didn't even hear it when it hit the ground. My hands met the heavy red fabric of Emily's banner, and I winced as some of the sharp baubles lacerated my skin. All the breath in my lungs came out in a tortured sigh, and my body flattened against the wall.

Harsh hands grabbed hold of my shoulders and spun me around, driving me forcefully into the wall once more. I didn't even feel the banner's baubles and doodads poke my flesh this time. I had other things to worry about.

I was looking into Pete's irate countenance, his eyes aglow with rage now. It seemed his entire body was shaking with barely concealed emotion, and I knew it wouldn't take much for him to snap and kill me right there.

A few feet away, safely out of the danger zone, Alex leaned against the railing, frowning. He had to realize Pete was crazy and dangerous. He'd told Pete it was a mistake to kill Sam Felber. Would he just stand idly by while Pete wrung my neck?

The only sound in the stairwell now was our breathing. Alex was making a clucking sound with his tongue, like a hen, and I wondered if that was the way he dealt with stress.

"You know," Pete told me with contempt in his voice, "I knew you were trouble from the moment I saw you. Just the way you looked at me made it obvious. You prejudiced?"

"Against murderers?" I asked. "Yes, I guess I am." I lifted my chin in defiance, waiting.

He pulled back a hand, ready to strike me, and I pinched my eyes shut when the stairwell door opened one flight above. The heavy metal hinges gave their usual creak of protest. No sound was ever sweeter.

Pete froze, lowering his hand. Alex craned his neck to see who it was. I took a firm grip on the edges of the huge banner on the wall behind me.

There was a footstep, and then Duncan's voice called out, "Rose? Rose, are you there?"

Pete's look warned me not to answer, and I obeyed.

More feet scuffled overhead, and we heard Lily say, "She should have been back ages ago, Duncan. I think we'd better check the archives."

When Pete turned to Alex for advice, facing away from me, I made my move. Grasping the edge of the banner, I jerked hard, stepping away as the huge piece of material fell from the wall.

"Sorry, Emily," I apologized.

It crumpled slowly, falling over Pete's head and enveloping him in red felt. Pete gave a shout of bewilderment and protest and put up his hands, struggling to dislodge the heavy material.

Alex, stunned, looked on wide-eyed as I hollered for help. Almost immediately Lily and Duncan could be heard scrambling down the steps.

What a sight must have greeted them! Pete encased in red banner, fumbling around to try to escape it, me shoving at him ineffectually in an effort to keep him in one place, and Alex, now shocked into motion, making quickly for the exit below.

Lily gasped and threw in with me, pummeling with both hands and kicking out with her pointy-toed shoes. Her wiry strength served us well. Together we backed him into the corner and continued our assault.

Looking for some sort of weapon, I reached for my shoe. Not high heeled like Lily's, but flat, with a nice, heavy heel that made a good hammer.

Duncan, seeing Alex attempting to flee, charged past us in hot pursuit. He reacted like a movie stuntman, launching himself down the stairs onto Alex's shoulders. In the seconds before they connected, he looked like a skydiver, all four limbs stretched out to their fullest. Then there was a crash, and I cringed as they hit the hard ground. I could hear the two men grunting as all the air was knocked out of them. Duncan had landed full onto Alex, now collapsed beneath him. After a few half-hearted struggles, the lawyer was still. Just for good measure, Duncan gave him a shake to rattle his teeth and sat up.

Looking to us, he gasped out a question. "You okay?"

I nodded. "I'm fine. But they were going to kill me! He killed Sam Felber." I poked the red bundle. "And the treaty's a fake! And they were going to build a mall!" I babbled on in a rush, the words tumbling over one another in the hurry to get out.

"What?" Lily wrinkled up her nose, her hands pressing hard against Pete. She looked incredulous, eyebrows shot up, cheeks flushed from exertion. "A mall?"

"It's a long story, Lil, and I'll be glad to tell it," I promised, "but first we need the police."

It was well after midnight. Duncan and I were holed up in the student lounge on the lower level, sipping vending-machine coffee. The police had come and gone, taking Alex and Pete with them, along with a statement from me.

Duncan had kept one foot on Alex's back and opened the stairwell door, shouting down the corridor in the direction of the lounge. As I'd hoped, it was inhabited, and it had been Karen who responded to Duncan's call, racing off to get the authorities.

In no time the stairwell had filled with people— police, board members, and curious students—and the next hour or so will always be a blur to me. A jumble of faces and thousands of questions.

Dr. Brossman had just sighed in resignation when he saw me, giving his head a shake. Even if I worked here for the next twenty years and they were totally uneventful, he'd always label me a troublemaker, I knew. But I didn't care.

Lily and Duncan looked on as the police listened to my story, taking notes and making me repeat myself over and over. An investigative team went up to the archives, dusting for prints and looking for evidence to support my words.

Alex had played it cool, using all the lawyer lingo he possessed to not say a word. Pete remained silent throughout, glowering at me. He looked a bit worse for wear, a few bruises already coloring his skin. There was a cut about an inch long on one cheek, beaded with a thin line of dried blood. My heel must have caught him there, I decided.

After I'd finished my narrative, detailing Pete and Alex's plan to get the land by claiming treaty rights, one police officer had been moved to comment. Turning to Pete, he asked, "How could you do it? Betray your people like that for personal gain?"

Pete scowled. "Hey, you folks had Christopher Columbus—and you celebrate it, man!"

I looked to Duncan. He was taking this hard, perhaps hardest of all. So idealistic, so driven by a need for justice, he'd just run headfirst into the real world. It was painful to watch. He had his head down, studying the floor and rocking back and forth on his heels. Slipping my arm around his waist, I gave him a cuddle and a kiss on the earlobe. When he looked over at me, he gave a weak smile, one corner of his mouth going up in that dear, lopsided fashion.

"I'm okay," he told me in a quiet voice. "Really."

Now, hours later, he took another swig of that strong black solution that passed for coffee and heaved a great sigh. Lily had long since left for home, but we had remained behind.

He covered my hand with his, fingering one of the scrapes I'd gotten from the bejeweled banner. "I'm just so glad we went looking for you. Sorry we waited as long as we did."

His voice was like a caress, soft and flowing, and I felt my body respond to his concern and affection. Tears flooded my eyes, and I blinked them away, feeling foolish and emotional. To cover up, I pressed a kiss into the palm of his hand and gushed like a movie heroine, "My hero!"

Duncan's cheeks colored, and he gave a grim smile. My thoughts remained serious, though, and I watched Duncan stirring his coffee.

We'd had an adventure. We'd solved a crime. We'd worked well together. For the first time in my life, I was content. Not antsy to move on or avoid any commitment. This was new and exciting for me. Uncharted territory. I needed to put it on the map.

"Duncan," I began slowly, setting my own spoon in motion. "Are you happy?"

His eyes grew wide, and I knew my question's hidden agenda was revealed. "Yes," he said, his lips fighting a smile. "I'd say I'm very happy. What about you? Like your job? Going to stick around a while?"

I was already nodding my head, stirring my coffee faster and faster until the liquid sloshed over the rim of my cup and puddled all around. I let the spoon clatter onto the table and clasped my hands together in my lap. My heart seemed to pound and skip beats at the same time as I dangled on an emotional precipice, knowing we were at a crossroads and glad to be there.

Duncan laughed at my discomfiture, and I scowled at him good-naturedly.

"I hope Lunham College will survive with the two of us teamed up," he told me, his hand stealing over to grasp mine. Pulling me toward him, he held my eyes, showing me humor and affection and a sparkle I knew I'd always treasure.

I let the love I felt for him shine through, warming my heart and tingling my cheeks. My eyelids fluttered shut as Duncan drew within a hair's breadth.

Then, ah, then, he kissed me, and I knew I'd found my way home at last—and was here to stay.